Gemini

Annabelle Starr

EGMONT

Special thanks to:

Rachel Rimmer, St John's Walworth Church of England School and Belmont Primary School

EGMONT
We bring stories to life

Published in Great Britain 2007
by Egmont UK Limited
239 Kensington High Street, London W8 6SA

Text & illustrations © 2007 Egmont UK Ltd
Text by Rachel Rimmer
Illustrations by Helen Turner

ISBN 978 1 4052 3244 9

3 5 7 9 10 8 6 4 2

A CIP catalogue record for this title is available
from the British Library

Typeset by Avon DataSet Ltd, Bidford on Avon, Warwickshire
Printed and bound in Great Britain by the CPI Group

Meet the Megastar Mysteries Team!

Hi, this is me, **Rosie Parker** (otherwise known as Nosy Parker), and these are my best mates . . .

. . . **Soph** (Sophie) **McCoy** – she's a real fashionista sista – and . . .

. . . **Abs** (Abigail) **Flynn**, who's officially une grande genius.

Here's my mum, **Liz Parker**.
Much to my embarrassment,
her fashion and music taste
is well and truly stuck in the
1980s (but despite all that
I still love her dearly) . . .

. . . and my nan,
Pam Parker, the murder-
mystery freak I mentioned
on the cover. Sometimes,
just sometimes, her crackpot
ideas do come in handy.

Consider yourself introduced!

Rosie's Mini Megastar Phrasebook

Want to speak our lingo, but don't know your soeurs from your signorinas? No problemo! Just use my comprehensive guide . . .

-a-rama	add this ending to a word to indicate a large quantity: e.g. 'The after-show party was celeb-a-rama'
amigo	Spanish for 'friend'
au contraire, mon frère	French for 'on the contrary, my brother'
au revoir	French for 'goodbye'
barf/barfy/barfissimo	sick/sick-making/very sick-making indeed
bien sûr, ma soeur	French for 'of course, my sister'
bon	French for 'good'
bonjour	French for 'hello'
celeb	short for 'celebrity'
convo	short for 'conversation'
cringe-fest	a highly embarrassing situation
Cringeville	a place we all visit from time to time when something truly embarrassing happens to us
cringeworthy	an embarrassing person, place or thing might be described as this
daggy	Australian for 'unfashionable' or unstylish'
doco	short for 'documentary'
exactamundo	not a real foreign word, but a great way to express your agreement with someone
exactement	French for 'exactly'

excusez moi	French for 'excuse me'
fashionista	'a keen follower of fashion' – can be teamed with 'sista' for added rhyming fun
glam	short for 'glamorous'
gorge/gorgey	short for 'gorgeous': e.g. 'the lead singer of that band is gorge/gorgey'
hilarioso	not a foreign word at all, just a great way to liven up 'hilarious'
hola, señora	Spanish for 'hello, missus'
hottie	no, this is *not* short for hot water bottle – it's how you might describe an attractive-looking boy to your friends
-issimo	try adding this ending to English adjectives for extra emphasis: e.g. coolissimo, crazissimo – très funissimo, non?
je ne sais pas	French for 'I don't know'
je voudrais un beau garçon, s'il vous plaît	French for 'I would like an attractive boy, please'
journos	short for 'journalists'
les Français	French for, erm, 'the French'
Loserville	this is where losers live, particularly evil school bully Amanda Hawkins
mais	French for 'but'
marvelloso	not technically a foreign word, just a more exotic version of 'marvellous'
massivo	Italian for 'massive'
mon amie/mes amis	French for 'my friend'/'my friends'
muchos	Spanish for 'many'

non	French for 'no'
nous avons deux garçons ici	French for 'we have two boys here'
no way, José!	'that's never going to happen!'
oui	French for 'yes'
quelle horreur!	French for 'what horror!'
quelle surprise!	French for 'what a surprise!'
sacré bleu	French for 'gosh' or even 'blimey'
stupido	this is the Italian for 'stupid' – stupid!
-tastic	add this ending to any word to indicate a lot of something: e.g. 'Abs is braintastic'
très	French for 'very'
swoonsome	decidedly attractive
si, si, signor/signorina	Italian for 'yes, yes, mister/miss'
terriblement	French for 'terribly'
une grande	French for 'a big' – add the word 'genius' and you have the perfect description of Abs
Vogue	it's only the world's most influential fashion magazine, darling!
voilà	French for 'there it is'
what's the story, Rory?	'what's going on?'
what's the plan, Stan?	'which course of action do you think we should take?'
what the crusty old grandads?	'what on earth?'
zut alors!	French for 'darn it!'

Hi Megastar reader!

My name's Annabelle Starr*. I'm a fashion stylist – just like Soph's Aunt Penny – which means it's my job to help celebrities look their best at all times.

Over the years, I've worked with all sorts of big names, some of whom also have seriously big egos! Take the time I flew all the way to Japan to style a shoot for a girl band. One of the members refused to wear the designer number I'd picked out for her and insisted on sporting a dress her mum had run up from some revolting old curtains instead. The only way I could get her to take it off was to persuade her it didn't match her pet Pekinese's outfit!

Anyway, when I first started out, I never dreamt I'd write a series of books based around my crazy celebrity experiences, but that's just what I've done with Megastar Mysteries. Rosie, Soph and Abs have just the sort of adventures I wish my friends and I could have got up to when we were teenagers!

I really hope you enjoy reading the books as much as I enjoyed writing them!

Love **Annabelle**

* I'll let you in to a little secret: this isn't my real name, but in this business you can never be too careful!

PRODUCTION *Gemini*

DIRECTOR *Robert D. Squire*

DATE *03/04*

SCENE *Big Night Out*

TAKE *17*

CAMERA *Greg*

Chapter One

I owe Soph's Aunt Penny, big time! And I'm talking SERIOUSLY big time – not just, like, the favour you owe your mate who distracted the teacher so you didn't have to answer that awkward question. No, Penny is très marvelloso with sequins on top. Basically, she totally rocks! Firstly, she's nice and always talks to me, Soph and Abs like we're normal people, not annoying kids (even though Soph drives her mad, asking about the latest fashion goss). Secondly, she looks like a rock star with her skinny jeans and cool T-shirts.

Thirdly, she is a fashion stylist and knows EVERYONE there is to know. And finally, most importantly, she's styling Australia's most famous and gorgeous teen actresses, the Sweetland twins, on their first film, which is being shot in London. Oh, yes, and SHE'S GOT ME, ABS AND SOPH JOBS AS RUNNERS ON THE SET!!!

As soon as we heard that Penny was going to be working on the film, about a month before Easter, Soph started begging her to get us on set somehow. We knew it was a long shot, but as Abs pointed out, the opportunity to meet megastars like the Sweetlands doesn't tend to come along regularly. Every day we'd ask Soph for news and every day she'd shake her head sadly. 'Penny said she'd see what she can do,' was the best she could manage.

And then, the evening after school broke up for Easter, when we were all looking forward to a long holiday filled with mad family members and wandering round boring old Borehurst, Soph instant-messaged me and Abs:

FashionPolice: Guess what!!!

CutiePie: You've come up with a new smock design and Topshop are going to stock it?

FashionPolice: Oh, ha, ha. Very funny, Abs. You wait – one day I will *rule* the fashion shelves. Or rails. Whatever. Anyway, guess again.

NosyParker: Meanie Greenie rang you up and said, actually, don't do all that homework this holiday, Soph. And tell Abs and Rosie not to bother either.

FashionPolice: Nope. Penny rang and said we could go on the set!!!

NosyParker: YOU LIE!!!

FashionPolice: Au contraire, mon frère. And it's even better than that!

CutiePie: What could be better than going on a film set and meeting the Sweetland twins?!

FashionPolice: We'll be there for two weeks. She's got us jobs as runners!!!

NosyParker: AAAAAAAAAAAAAAAAAAA
AAAAAAAAAAAAAAAAAAAARGH!
CutiePie: AAAAAAAAAAAAAAAAAAAAA
AAAAAAAAAAAAAAAARGH!

Imagine – two weeks on a film set! This was so going to be the best Easter holiday ever!

While I was doing a victory dance in my bedroom, Nan popped her head round the door.

'You all right, Rosie love?' she asked. 'There's a heck of a lot of banging about going on.'

'Nan! I'm going to be a runner!!!' I shrieked, grabbing her hands and trying to get her to do a jig with me. 'How cool is that?'

'A runner? But I thought you hated PE?' Nan said, confused.

I burst out giggling. Who cared about anything else – I was going to be working in the film industry!

❋　❋　❋

And now we were on the train on the way to Penny's flat, accompanied by Soph's mum. Soph had my copy of *Star Secrets* magazine and was testing me on my knowledge of the twins. I buy *Star Secrets* every week and what I don't know about most celebs isn't worth knowing. If only there were a lesson at school where I could apply this knowledge. But no, we have to stick to boring old maths and French and the like. Yawn-o-rama.

'OK, so what's Paige's favourite colour?' Soph asked me.

'Blue,' I replied, rolling my eyes at the easy-peasiness of the question.

'What was the name of Shelby's first crush?' asked Abs, peering at the quiz over Soph's shoulder.

'Jonathan Appleby,' I said.

'Their characters' middle names in *Hart Grove*?' Soph said.

'Amy and Kate,' I crowed.

'Their star sign?'

'Gemini – duh!'

'OK, OK, we give up. You know everything there is to know about Paige and Shelby

Sweetland,' Abs sighed.

'Yes! I told you I did!' I punched the air with glee. Abs made a big 'loser' sign at me.

'Girls!' said Soph's mum, looking round the train carriage with embarrassment. She had volunteered to escort us to London, but I think she was regretting it. 'Remember what Aunt Penny said – you've got to treat them like ordinary people.'

'Yeah, OK, Mum,' Soph said. 'But they're not ordinary, are they? I mean, *ordinary* people don't star in a soap opera their whole lives!'

'*Ordinary* people don't star in their own film when they're only sixteen!' Abs pointed out.

Mrs McCoy rolled her eyes. 'Remember, you're there to do a job. Don't go all starry-eyed – you'll put Penny in a difficult position. She stuck her neck out to get you these runner jobs, so you've got to work hard.'

'We know, Mum!' Soph said. 'We'll be good. Although I don't know about Rosie. She always starts babbling rubbish when we meet celebrities.'

'I do not!' I protested. 'Well, OK, I do sometimes. But you make it sound as if we meet them all the time. Which we don't.'

'Unlike Penny,' said Soph enviously. 'I'm so going to be a stylist before I become a designer – you get to meet *everyone*.'

'Don't forget that *we've* met Mirage Mullins, who's a proper megastar number-one chart sensation,' Abs pointed out. 'And Rosie's got Maff from Fusion's number . . .'

I went red. It was true. Maff – the lead singer of a totally cool band – had been my first kiss. He's totally gorge *and* a pop star! In fact, since we'd last seen one another, Fusion had got into the Top 40 – so he was totally famous too!

'It's not like he's my boyfriend,' I said.

'Only in your dreams,' Soph sighed. Seriously, sometimes Soph is so soppy, it's worrying.

Mrs McCoy sighed too. She was getting embarrassed by us being noisy (she actually has a sense of what is embarrassing and what isn't, unlike some mothers I could mention), but honestly, I don't know how she expected us to be quiet and sensible. Obviously, normally we were nice, well-behaved girls, a credit to our parents and our school – well, mostly. But hello?? We were going to meet Paige and Shelby Sweetland!!! The only thing that could have made it better was if Amanda Hawkins, our arch-enemy from school, had known about it. It would have been seriously good to have spent the whole last day at school being very, very smug. But it would be even better to tell her about it after we had met them. I couldn't wait to see Amanda's face after the Easter holidays!

'What do runners do, anyway?' I asked.

'Oh, just run messages and stuff about. You know, be helpful on the set,' Abs said knowledgeably.

'Ah. I can do that. I'm good at that,' I said. Imagine, I was going to meet the Sweetland twins – maybe even become their friend – and all I had to do was be helpful! This was going to be good.

Just then, the train driver announced we were coming into the station. London, here we come!

I am so planning to live in London when I become a top celebrity reporter. Penny's flat was coolissimo! It was really small, but it had amazing views of the city and she'd decorated it really nicely – loads of cream furniture and funky accessories. It looked like it was straight out of a magazine. Abs, Soph and I were going to share the spare room, for two whole weeks!! Good old Soph – her powers of persuasion were just getting better and better. One day, she might even convince my nan to wear one of her fashion creations.

When we arrived, Soph's mum and Penny had a cup of tea and a chat, while me, Abs and Soph ran from room to room, imagining it was our flat and we all lived there together. We made a pact to live together when Soph is a fashion queen, like her aunt, and I'm a celeb reporter and Abs is . . . well, whatever she wants to be! That's something I love about her – she's so brainy. She says she's currently keeping her options open. I think she'd make a good detective. Or maybe prime minister.

Before Mrs McCoy left, she made each of us promise about a million times to be good and do what Penny told us and not get into any trouble – over and over again – while we nodded. As soon as the door closed behind her, we sat Penny down to ask her about Paige and Shelby.

'Is it true they can read each other's minds?' I asked.

'What? No!' Penny laughed.

'Oh. Well, what are they like? Are they really snobby?' asked Soph.

Before Penny could answer, Abs jumped in. 'I reckon they're really nice. They always seem down to earth in interviews. But is it hard to tell them apart?'

'Do they choose their own clothes?' Soph asked.

'Well –' Penny began.

'I can't believe we're going to meet them!' I squealed.

'I know! This is the best Easter ever!' Soph and

Abs said at exactly the same time. Well, it was!

'Girls, girls, calm down,' said Penny. 'Now, I know you're really excited, but you've got to play it cool. Paige and Shelby *are* very nice and you should treat them as ordinary people, not huge stars. They're just teenagers like you, you know.'

'I sooo believe you,' Soph said, wide-eyed and innocent.

'Well, they are! And when you're on set, remember that you're at the bottom of the ladder, and you must do whatever anyone asks you to do – and quickly.'

'Just like my Saturday job at the salon,' Soph said, nodding. She worked every weekend at the Dream Beauty salon, but she'd taken time off over Easter to be on the film set.

'You'll probably have to do things like get coffees and take memos around the set and so on. Remember the three Ps: be polite, be punctual and be personable.'

We looked blankly at Penny. Person-*what*?

'Personable means friendly,' Penny smiled.

'Film sets are fun, but people will get cross with you if you get in the way.'

'No problemo. You'll hardly know we're there,' Abs said. 'So how big an entourage do Paige and Shelby have?'

Penny shrugged. 'I don't know – there are quite a few people working for them. I'm their stylist, of course. And they have a hairdresser. They've even got their own astrologer!'

'Really?' I asked. 'Someone tells them their horoscope every day?'

'Yes,' Penny said. 'They're really into all that.'

'Hey, what does Destiny Blake say for Pisces this week?' Soph said.

I flicked to the horoscopes page in *Star Secrets* to read what their astrologer had predicted. 'You will meet new people, so stay open to new experiences. And give your friends your last bit of chocolate.'

'Oh, ha, ha,' Soph said, grabbing *Star Secrets* from me. 'Well, Sagittarians should watch out for trouble coming their way apparently. So that's you warned if you nick my chocolate.'

'I wonder if any other celeb has a personal astrologer?' Abs said.

'I can't think of anyone,' I mused. Then I gasped. 'They're setting a new trend – right under our noses!'

'Soon no one will be able to do anything without consulting their astrologer! There'll be chaos in celeb world if anything happens to the stargazers!' Abs said.

'Hmm,' Penny said. 'Well, Paige and Shelby's astrologer is certainly influential. They listen to everything she says. Not that that's always a good idea.'

'Why? What do you mean?' I asked.

'Oh, nothing. Just that she seems to have quite a hold on their careers. They hardly make a decision without her. It's a shame, because they're clever girls and they can think for themselves. After all, they've been in the business for years. But their astrologer's a bit odd sometimes.'

'Really?' I breathed. 'Does she make them stay in bed every Friday the thirteenth and stuff like that?'

'Oh, I don't know really,' Penny said, suddenly

looking a bit edgy. 'Anyway, I shouldn't be saying all this. It's very unprofessional of me. And please don't go on about how weird it is to the twins. They're a bit sensitive about her.' Penny checked her amazingly cool diver's watch. 'Oh, look at the time. Right, girls, we've got a very early start. We've got to be on set at six-thirty, and I imagine you want some beauty sleep.'

'We're about to meet two of the most beautiful teen stars in the world. Of *course* we want some beauty sleep!' Soph said. 'And I've got to decide what to wear!'

'Good grief. Right, we definitely need to get to bed now then!' Penny said, winking at Abs and me.

'Last one in bed's a Z-list celeb,' I shouted, running to the bathroom.

'Night, girls!' Penny called.

Tomorrow we were going to meet Paige and Shelby Sweetland! I couldn't wait!

Chapter Two

Top ten things not to do when you're on a film set:

1. Trip over some wires – they could be attached to a très important camera.
2. Say, 'wow . . . wow . . . wow . . . ' the whole time as you walk around staring at everything.
3. Instantly forget what Penny is telling you about where the coffee and breakfast things are located because you're gawping at the amount of make-up in the make-up room.

4. Touch anything.

5. Talk to anyone – unless they talk to you first.

6. Walk in front of a camera. (Duh. Soph and I almost did – but luckily someone shouted at us in time.)

7. Try on a wig from the costume department. (Even if Abs did look hilarious dolled up like Gwen Stefani.)

8. Walk past the male star's dressing room a hundred times an hour, hoping to catch a glimpse of him.

9. Pick up a tennis ball and throw it to your friend, not realising it's a prop.

10. Try to talk to the main stars' astrologer.

So, we got to the swanky Hotel Londonia at the crack of dawn. I can't believe anyone gets anywhere at 6.30 in the morning and looks even vaguely awake, let alone camera-ready, but I guess that's what the make-up artist is for. Soph had spent ages working out her outfit, and settled on something quite normal, for her: a short skirt with boots, a big yellow hand-knitted jumper that practically hid the skirt, and a red beret. Abs and I were just in jeans and T-shirts. We knew we couldn't begin to compete with Soph, let alone two megastar actresses.

The hotel was HUMONGOUS. The film people had basically taken it over and it was packed with stuff: pieces of scenery, lights, cameras, props – you name it, it was there. And there were loads of people running about doing stuff. I had no idea what, but it all looked important.

Penny led us straight to the dressing rooms after getting us security passes. I felt so important. It had my name on it and everything: 'Rosie Parker: *Gemini*: Security Pass Level 2.' Level 2. Not Level 1. Level 2, which was probably way more important – unless Level 1 was actually better. I started to peer at everyone else's pass to try to work it out.

As Penny knocked on the door that said 'Paige and Shelby Sweetland', Me, Soph and Abs all looked at each other and took a deep breath. This was it!

'Come in!' said a very familiar voice. It was Paige!!! Or maybe Shelby!!! (I've never been able to tell their voices apart. They really are *identical* twins.)

We went in and there they were, sitting on a cream sofa in matching dressing gowns and the charm bracelets they're famous for always wearing. They jumped up and hugged Penny. They looked amazing, despite the early morning. Their long dark hair was shiny, and they were tanned from the Australian sun. Even at that distance, I couldn't tell which was which. Paige had a mole on her forehead, above her eyebrow, but if you couldn't see that, you couldn't tell them apart at all! It must be so weird looking exactly the same as someone else. I bet Soph would hate it. Although, being Soph, even if she had an identical twin I bet she'd find some way to make herself look different.

'Paige, Shelby, I want you to meet our new

runners,' Penny said. 'This is my niece, Sophie, and these are her friends, Rosie and Abigail.'

'Cool hat,' Paige (I thought) said admiringly, as she shook Soph's hand.

'G'day, nice to meet you guys,' Shelby (I guessed) said, shaking hands with Abs and me.

'Hi! It's really nice to meet you,' I said back, trying to act all cool. It was really them!

'It's amazing to be here,' Soph gushed. 'Do you know what you two are going to wear today?' Trust Soph to get straight in there with fashion talk!

'No way, mate – that's Penny's job! But we do have some ideas. Hey, grab a seat,' Shelby said, gesturing to the sofa.

Me, Abs and Soph all sat down in a row and gazed at the twins. They perched on stools in front of huge mirrors while Penny rushed about, getting various outfits ready for them. There were rails and rails of clothes in the room – all colour-coordinated so Penny could find stuff easily. And there were rows and rows and rows of shoes. If the twins hadn't been in the room, Soph wouldn't have been able to resist rifling through everything there and trying it all on.

'Do you like wearing the same outfits as each other?' she asked them.

'Well, sometimes it's fun,' Shelby said, glancing at Paige. 'And we have to for this movie in a few scenes. But we prefer to be individuals really.'

Paige nodded in agreement, then asked, 'How long are you going to be working with us?'

'Just a couple of weeks,' I said.

'Oh, you'll see a lot in two weeks,' said Shelby. 'Of the movie, I mean. We're shooting quite a few crucial scenes next. That's why it's so important that we don't look daggy.'

'Yeah, you'd better choose nice stuff,' Paige said to Penny, pretending to be stern.

There was a knock at the door. 'Morning!' said a voice and a very pretty woman came into the dressing room, followed by a guy with cropped ginger hair.

'Hi, Melissa,' Paige and Shelby said. (Wow,

they even spoke together, they were so coordinated!) 'Melissa, these are our new runners – Sophie, Abigail and Rosie. Girls, this is Melissa, our make-up artist, and the guy with her is Felipe, who does our hair.'

'Hi, girls,' Melissa said, smiling.

Felipe had gone straight to Paige's hair and was twirling it in his hand. 'Terrible! We will have to wash it again!' he said, throwing his hands up in despair. Then, turning to us, he said, 'Hello, ladies.'

I smoothed my embarrassingly messy hair. If he thought Paige's hair was bad, he'd probably think my bird's nest was grossissimo.

'I'm glad I'm wearing a hat,' Soph whispered.

'Girls, why don't you get everyone their breakfast?' Penny said from behind the huge pile of tops she was carrying. 'Take people's orders and bring it all back here. Oh, and get something for Misty too.'

'Who's Misty?' I asked, looking around. 'Is she your dog?' I was sort of hoping the twins would have a pet I could mind – a Chihuahua maybe, or a Labradoodle. Penny, Melissa and Felipe burst out laughing, but stopped when they noticed the twins weren't smiling.

'No,' Paige said. 'Misty Van Deville is our astrologer.'

PLEASE, GROUND, OPEN UP AND SWALLOW ME. LIKE, NOW.

I had gone bright red. Even so, I carried on, ignoring a glare from Penny. 'So why do you have an astrologer?'

'Well, we've known Misty since we were young . . .' Paige said.

'And she's basically made us who we are today,' Shelby finished. 'We consult her on everything – boys, scripts, outfits . . . She's the secret of our success! In fact, she suggested we make this movie.'

'Wow!' Soph said. 'So you really believe in all that stuff – star signs, planets, horoscopes?'

Just then, the door opened and a blonde woman wearing a purple trouser suit and a pink scarf walked in. Her perfume practically walked in too, it was so strong. Abs, who has a super-sensitive nose, began to choke and her eyes streamed with tears. It was really obvious because everyone in the room had gone quiet.

'Hi, Misty,' Paige said brightly. 'These are our new runners. We were just chatting. They're going to get us some breakfast.'

Misty's eyebrows shot up to her hairline. 'Chatting?' she said.

Oh, joy. She was obviously not happy.

'They're taking orders,' Shelby put in. 'What would you like for breakfast, Misty?'

'A skinny latte and a raisin bagel,' Misty said, sitting down at a table and not even looking at us.

'Er, OK,' I said. 'Melissa and Felipe, what would you like?'

They gave us their orders, and Penny told us hers. How the crusty old grandads do waitresses remember everything? Oh, yeah, they write stuff down. I had to remember to bring a pencil and paper the next day . . .

'And what would you like, Paige?' Abs asked.

Paige opened her mouth, but Misty cut in. 'They'll both have an iced tea and a cereal bar,' she said, not looking up from the script she was studying.

Shelby said, 'I was thinking about a bacon sandwich this morning . . .'

Misty looked at her. 'I think a cereal bar would be better, don't you? I predict that it's going to be a tough day and you don't want to be bloated.'

Shelby shrugged her shoulders. 'OK,' she said.

Abs, Soph and I looked at each other. Wow. *That* was control.

'I think you've got everyone's orders now?' Misty said in the general direction of the sofa we were sitting on. 'Please hurry back with everything. We've got a lot to get through today.'

What an attitude! We immediately got up and scurried off. Penny gave us a *see-what-I-mean?* kind of look as we left.

'Paige and Shelby are sooo nice!' Abs said.

'They liked my hat!' Soph said, preening.

'But what is that Misty woman's problem?' I muttered, checking no one could hear me. 'She's so not what I imagined an astrologer to be like.'

'Yeah,' Abs said thoughtfully. 'She's . . . different somehow.'

'Well, she's obviously trying hard *not* to be different,' Soph said.

We looked at her, confused.

'Well, you can tell by the scarf and the earrings, can't you?'

'Er, what??' I asked. Never mind astrology, Soph can read people's minds just by checking out their shoes.

'Didn't you notice? She's wearing a really expensive trouser suit and then she puts this horrible floaty scarf and naff dangly earrings with it. I mean, who would do that?' Soph was clearly horrified by this très serious fashion error.

'I don't get it,' Abs said with a frown.

'I think she's trying to dress like people think an astrologer should – all new-age and floaty and unfashionable – but she actually likes wearing posh stuff,' Soph explained.

'OK, whatever,' I said. 'The main thing is that Paige and Shelby are poppets!'

'I can't believe we get to spend two weeks with them!' Abs said.

'Yeah, but if Misty's going to be there the whole time, I predict it's going to be boring,' I said, imitating the astrologer's mystical drawl. 'She's not very friendly.'

'I know, but hello? We're on a film set!! How much more the opposite of boring could that be?' said Soph.

She was right. No matter how odd their astrologer was, I had a feeling spending time with Paige and Shelby Sweetland was not going to be dull.

Chapter Three

After our first day on set, I called home. Mum and Nan had made me promise to tell them all about it.

'Paige and Shelby are so nice!' I said. 'And so gorgeous. I wish my hair would look like theirs.' Some hope. Swingy, glossy, film-star hair versus a long stringy blonde mop – no contest.

'Now, Rosie. Your hair is lovely,' Nan said. I immediately perked up, even though I know nans are *supposed* to say stuff like that, even if it isn't true. 'And anyway, I bet they have lots of people fussing over them all day. I mean, if they need someone to tell them what to *wear*, then they obviously need people to do their hair as well . . .'

Nan has never really got what Penny's job is. I've tried to explain that stylists find all the clothes and shoes and work with the director on the 'look' for the film, but she doesn't understand. Mind you, her heroine is Jessica Fletcher from *Murder, She Wrote*, who only ever wears cardigans and sturdy shoes, so I might have been expecting too much.

'They've got loads of people working with them,' I said. 'They've got a stylist, a hairdresser, a make-up artist and an astrologer.'

'A what?' Nan said.

'An astrologer. You know, like "this week you will find love in a holiday park." That kind of thing,' I said.

'Oooh, hee, hee,' Nan giggled. I'd made her go all coy. She'd met a chap called Gerry the previous summer at the holiday camp where I'd met swoonsome Maff from Fusion. She'd done better than me – she'd seen Gerry three times since then and I'd seen Maff no times. Still, that's the deal with celebs – they are so busy, they can't keep in contact with ordinary schoolgirls. Sigh. This is why pensioners make better boyfriends than pop stars do. (But it's the only reason.)

Anyway, Nan passed me over to Mum at that point and went off to have a calming cup of tea and a bourbon cream.

'So what's the plot of the film?' Mum asked. 'Is there a scene with a band or a singer? You could mention me, you know.' Sacré bleu! She is so embarrassing. Cringe-issimo, in fact. Just because she's in this eighties tribute band, the Banana Splits, and performs in the pubs in our area. (You can tell from that how cool Borehurst is.) Now she thinks she's ready to be in a film! Honestly!!!

'Mum, not everyone likes Bananarama's music, you know. Anyway, I don't know the whole plot yet. We haven't seen the script. They only filmed one scene today and it was just the twins in their bedroom, having a conversation.'

'Oh. Well, I hope you're being helpful,' she

said. 'How's Penny coping with you three staying in her flat?'

I glanced over at Penny, who was trying to write emails on her funky pink laptop while me, Soph and Abs were all shrieking on our mobiles to our families. 'She's fine. And we are being helpful, Mum.'

'Good. Nan wanted to know if you found the packet of custard creams she put in your bag for emergencies.'

'I found them this morning – all crushed into tiny pieces. Tell her thanks, though, and I'm pretty sure I'll be able to get a packet here in London, if I need to. Anyway, gotta go now.'

'OK, love. And remember, if there's an eighties flashback or anything in the film . . .'

'I'll let you know. Bye!'

Zut alors! My family were madder than ever. At least I'd escaped for Easter. Soph was so *lucky* to have such a cool aunt.

'Megan says hi,' Abs reported, having ended her call. Megan's her five-year-old sister. She's very sweet, but she's obsessed with dolls and dressing up as a princess, so it's hard to find things to talk about with her.

'This is so great!' Soph cried. 'Now, what are we going to wear tomorrow?'

* * *

After the first day or two, Soph, Abs and I got very good at scurrying all over the set and we stopped gawking at everything so much. It was coolissimo, though. Melissa and Felipe chatted to us whenever they had a moment, telling us the goss from other films they'd worked on, and Felipe even curled my hair one afternoon!

We met the director, Robert, on the second day – Penny introduced us to him. He was a big burly man with grey hair and a beard, dressed all in black. He was sitting with a stressed-looking assistant, going over the script. Penny had told us that Misty often suggested changes at the last minute, according to what the planets had told her to do. No wonder the assistant looked stressed!

'Hello, darlings,' Robert said as he kissed our cheeks. 'A pleasure to have you here. Penny assured me you would be most helpful.'

'Absolutely, Robert,' she said, smiling at him. 'They're excellent at getting coffees already!'

'Would you like anything, sir?' I asked.

'Oh, call me Robert,' he said, laughing. 'And no thanks, I've got a drink here.'

'He's very nice,' I remarked as we followed Penny off to the dressing rooms.

'Yes,' Penny said. 'He's a sweetheart, actually. You're lucky he's in charge – most directors wouldn't even consider letting you work here.'

'Well, I think you work with some lovely people,' I said.

It was true; most people were really nice to us, especially once we remembered what their coffee order was. Me, Soph and Abs started to carry pencils and paper with us at all times, despite Penny laughing at us. We took it seriously. And since I'm going to be a celebrity reporter, I had to get used to scribbling furiously and listening carefully. After all, we were mixing with some top celebs, and you never knew what I might pick up!

I'd eventually managed to find out that *Gemini* was a comedy about the twins and their family and all the shenanigans they got up to on holiday in London. A lot of the plot was about mistaken identity, of course. They had a love interest, but he hardly came out of his dressing room unless he had a scene. He was revising for exams apparently. Bor-*ing*!

Loads of the scenes were filmed in the hotel. We spent a lot of time being quiet so they wouldn't pick up odd sounds. It was brilliant to watch, but I couldn't believe how many times the actors had to go over each scene to get it right. And they did the scenes in funny orders. First they'd do one where the twins knew their dad had been warning off the boy they liked, and then they'd do one where they didn't. All in the same day! Très confusing.

One morning we were watching a scene between Shelby and Paige when Abs started spluttering. Misty had arrived.

She went over to Robert and whispered in his ear.

'Cut!' he shouted, and turned to listen to her. Then he called the twins over. 'Darlings, that was marvellous. However, Misty has suggested a few small changes to the script. Look . . .'

'She is so interfering!' I whispered to Abs. She nodded, trying not to choke.

'You never know. It could make it better,' Soph said. 'The twins must trust her for a reason.'

'Hmm,' I said, not convinced.

The twins went back to their places and began again. And it wasn't better.

'This doesn't make any sense,' Abs whispered. 'Why would Paige be angry in this scene? Surely she should be upset?'

Misty, who was walking past us, heard this and frowned. She spun on her heel and went back to Robert.

'Cut!' he shouted again. Everyone looked cross. He listened to Misty, and this time his eyes lit up. 'Yes! Excellent! Girls, another tiny change . . .'

And this time Paige said her lines as if she was

upset, just as Abs had suggested! Misty gave us a sly smile as she walked past us again. The evil woman had stolen Abs's idea! I was beginning to suspect she wasn't as supportive as she pretended to be.

※   ※   ※

The film people hadn't filmed 'on location' in London yet. I was hoping they'd do that while we were still working there. Being in the hotel the whole time was a teensy bit boring. All we seemed to do was get food for people. At least if we went on location, we'd have to help transport everything, and do exciting stuff like . . . well, go and get lunch for people. Film people get hungry *a lot.*

We were totally used to being runners, but we still weren't brilliant at getting up so early, which didn't help when we had to get everyone's breakfast. I got Misty's order wrong once (before the pencil and paper), and she could have fried her own egg with the glare she gave me.

Paige and Shelby were really nice to us – although if Misty was there (which she usually was), they would have to resort to eyebrow waggling and the odd grin. She didn't like them talking to us, particularly Soph, who kept trying to have fashion conversations with them. Soph made us laugh by imitating her:

'Paige, come over here a minute – I feel that you need to sit quietly before the next scene . . . Shelby, I have some water for you. The stars told me you'd need hydration today . . . Girls! Shouldn't you be reading your scripts? There've been some changes due to the alignment of Saturn. Come along . . .'

Even Penny was hardly allowed to talk to them. In the mornings, while we were delivering breakfast, Penny would be trying to sort out their clothes for the day, but Misty would poke her nose in there, too.

'We've already discussed this, haven't we, girls?' she'd say. 'Shelby should always have some green in her outfit, and Paige some blue. It brings them good luck. So those jumpers won't do.'

And Paige and Shelby would just smile sympathetically at Penny and shrug while Penny's carefully chosen outfits were binned! Penny was brilliant at her job and the twins always looked great before that astrologer witch got involved.

'It's not fair! You're a fab stylist,' Soph fumed. 'Why do they always let her interfere?'

Penny smiled. 'It is rather annoying, but they're paying me good money, so I'll just have to grin and bear it. At least the girls are nice.'

'I think there's something strange about Misty,' Abs said thoughtfully.

'Yeah,' I said. 'She's always sticking her nose into everything.'

'Hello? Ms Pot, meet Ms Kettle,' said Soph. 'But yeah, I agree there's something weird about her. And it starts with her outfits. Followed by her perfume.'

'I practically choke every time she walks past,' Abs said, totally traumatised.

Penny looked worried. 'I know you love to know everything about celebrities, but please don't go nosing about. If you stir up trouble, I could lose my job.'

'Us? Stir up trouble?' Soph said innocently.

'Seriously, Soph,' Penny warned. 'We just have to accept that Misty Van Deville is here to stay, like it or not.'

'We definitely like it not,' Soph muttered.

✸ ✸ ✸

The day after this warning from Penny, I headed for the twins' dressing room to take their lunch orders. Part of me was very excited . . . BECAUSE I WAS ON A FILM SET WITH TWO OF THE BIGGEST TEEN STARS IN THE WORLD!!! Part of me was really hoping Misty wouldn't be with them. So I was dawdling a bit, trying to put off the moment when I'd have to see the Queen of the Zodiac, when I heard raised voices coming from their dressing room. I didn't want to interrupt anything, so I stopped to listen at the door. OK, so this was très nosy. But I didn't get the nickname Nosy Parker for nothing.

'Why would I want to read anything she has to say?' I was pretty sure that was Shelby shouting.

'Just listen, will you, Shelby! I've only read the first bit, but it sounds really genuine,' Paige replied. She sounded upset too.

'You reckon? Mum's never had anything genuine to say to us. Never!' Shelby cried.

'So if it's all rubbish, why was it in Misty's handbag? Why was she hiding it from us?'

'What were you doing in her handbag anyway?'

'I had a headache and I needed some aspirin. I thought Misty might have some. Look, what matters is that Mum's written to us, and –'

'I've *told* you, Paige. I don't want to hear anything she has to say!'

Wow! This was serious stuff! Serious – and private. There was no way I should have been listening to it. Just as I was thinking about knocking on the door, I smelt a familiar, horrible scent. I turned to see Misty at the end of the corridor. The last thing I wanted was for Misty to find me earwigging on the twins! I hurled myself into the dressing room next door, which was empty, luckily, so I didn't have to explain why I'd practically kicked the door down.

I heard Misty go into the twins' dressing room (without knocking – that's the kind of power she has!) and then I followed her. I knocked, of course.

'Come in!' Misty barked.

I opened the door. Paige and Shelby were sitting on the sofa, eating grapes. They smiled at me as I entered. They looked completely normal. It almost made me wonder if I'd been hearing things. Then I remembered that the twins were brilliant actresses.

'Er, I've come to take your lunch orders,' I said.

'Right. Three chicken salads and some mineral water,' Misty said.

'That sounds lovely,' Paige said.

'Yes, I really fancy chicken salad,' Shelby said.

I blinked. Why were they being so friendly to Misty? I mean, they were always polite, but usually they would wink at me or something as well. Today, they were acting as if her word was law.

'Is that all?' Misty enquired coldly, staring at me. I was obviously gaping at them all like a goldfish. A goldfish with bad hair.

'Er, yes. Three chicken salads coming up! No problemo,' I said, backing out of the room, confused.

Something was up. I knew it. I sniff out mysteries like Soph sniffs out bargains in a sale. And where there's a mystery, there's a need for someone to solve it – someone like moi. I hurried off to talk to Abs and Soph.

Chapter Four

That night, Penny was going out with a friend. She rooted around in a kitchen drawer to find a leaflet from a pizza-delivery place. She didn't trust us to cook without her being there, which was fair enough. After all, we *had* once set Abs's toaster on fire.

'How hard can it be to toast a bit of bread without burning down the kitchen?' Penny asked us.

'Honestly, it was like a freak accident or something,' I tried to explain.

'Yeah,' Abs said. 'It's a very temperamental toaster.'

'Right,' said Penny, clearly unconvinced. 'Anyway, pizza tonight, I think.'

I'd told the girls earlier I'd got something to tell them, but we had to wait till after Penny had left. I didn't want her to know I'd eavesdropped on the twins, even if I couldn't have helped overhearing them. I knew she wouldn't be pleased.

Soph and Abs had driven me mad all afternoon by continually whispering, 'What? What's going on? Tell us!' and passing me notes saying 'Two skinny lattes, one cheese toastie, TELL ME WHAT YOU KNOW!' so I made them wait until we'd got the pizza and were all sitting comfortably.

'Right, are you ready? When I went to get the twins' lunch order today, I just happened to overhear them having an argument –'

'Just happened to? We believe you, Nosy Parker!' Soph said.

'Honestly, I didn't mean to, but they were shouting. Anyway, it turns out Paige had found a letter from their mum in Misty's handbag. It was addressed to them but Misty had kept it!'

'No way, José! I knew there was something weird about her!' Abs said.

'Yeah, but listen, there's more. Paige wanted to read it but Shelby didn't. She kept saying she didn't want to hear anything from their mother. How weird is that?'

'That *is* odd,' Soph said. 'How come their mum is *writing* to them anyway?'

'Yeah, that's what I've been wondering,' Abs said. 'Where are their parents? I'm sure if their mum was here, she wouldn't let someone like Misty push them around. *My* mum wouldn't, anyway.'

'My mum wouldn't, either,' I said. 'Although she does love reading her stars. She's always convinced they're going to predict fame for the Banana Splits. Anyway, I'm sure I've read something about Paige and Shelby's mum. She used to be more involved, didn't she?'

'Let's look her up!' Soph said. 'We can check it out on Penny's laptop. She said we could use it for email if we wanted.'

'Good idea,' said Abs. 'Let's do a search for their mum.'

So we did. Straightaway, loads of links came up. They were all about the same thing. As soon as I started reading, the whole thing came back to me. I couldn't believe I'd forgotten the story.

Basically, Paige and Shelby's mum had been their manager for years. (Their father had walked out on them while they were babies, before they became famous. Serves him right!) But then, a few years ago, they'd discovered their earnings had pretty much disappeared. They didn't have any savings at all. This was mad, because they'd been on *Hart Grove* for ten years by then, and they'd done loads of adverts and stuff, so they should have had lots of money. It turned out they'd taken their mother to court and proved she had basically lost all their earnings, so they cut her out of their lives – 'divorced' her – and Misty became their legal guardian!!

'No wonder she has so much control over them,' Abs said, thoughtfully. 'If she's their guardian, they have to run everything past her while they're still under age.'

'Oooh, she's sneaky!' Soph said, almost dropping pizza on to the laptop, she was so outraged. 'I knew it!'

'You could say she's giving them a fresh start and a chance to forget all about their horrible mum.' I was still trying to see the positive side.

We looked at each other, then chorused, 'Nah!' Even though our mums were embarrassing (some more than others – Liz Parker was in the lead by a long way), we knew they'd never do anything to hurt us. It was unbelievable that a mother could steal from her daughters like that.

'Whatever happened with the twins' mum, there's definitely something très odd about Misty Van Deville,' Soph said.

'Oh, you're not still fixated on her, are you?' Penny had just got back and caught the tail-end of what Soph was saying.

'Penny, do you remember when the twins divorced their mother?' Abs asked.

'Yes,' Penny said, removing her laptop from the pizza danger zone before it got ruined. 'I was over in Australia working on *Hart Grove* at the time. It was all very shocking.'

'Why? What happened?' I probed.

'Well, it was Misty who'd found out that their mother was cheating them. The stars had told her so – and she helped the twins prove it. She guided them through the whole thing,' Penny said.

'Wow,' Abs said. 'No wonder they believe what she says.'

'Yup,' said Penny. 'None of the rest of us could believe it at first, because their mother was so nice and down to earth – like them – but you couldn't argue with the evidence. It was very sad.'

We all sighed, sympathetically.

'And the girls were very upset,' Penny recalled. 'They had to have a few weeks off work after the court case ended.'

'Oh, that was when their characters disappeared for a while, but it was never talked about on the show,' I said, remembering how it seemed strange at the time.

'Yeah,' Penny nodded. 'Anyway, Misty had been coming to the set more and more during the court case, and when the girls came back after their time off, they told us that she was going to be their guardian, so she would be there every day.'

'Didn't you find that really odd?' Abs asked. 'Don't they have any other relatives? I mean, who appoints their *astrologer* to be their guardian?!'

'Of course we thought it was odd. But the twins refused to talk about it, and you couldn't mention their mother to them or they'd burst into tears. Soon Misty banned everyone from speaking to them about anything apart from the next scene. Since they were the stars, the director went along with it. Everything was really tense.'

I gulped, 'Poor twins! How dire for them!'

'Anyway, that was a while ago. They're fine now. Although they've still got the dreaded Misty with them every day.' Penny made a face, then switched back to responsible-adult mode. 'Right. Time for bed, girls. It's another early start tomorrow.'

We got into our sleeping bags, but none of us could sleep. We were all thinking about the twins.

'There's something about this I don't understand,' Abs whispered finally.

'What?' I whispered back.

'Well, if they hate their mum so much, why are they arguing over this letter?'

'Yeah, and how come she's writing to them anyway?' said Soph.

'To say sorry?' I suggested.

'I think there's more to it than that,' Abs said. 'It's really unusual for the twins not to agree.'

'Yeah, that's true. They never argue. It says that in every interview I've read about them,' I said.

'So, something must be wrong. I think there's definitely more to this story. Let's investigate!' Abs said.

'Yeah!' Soph and I whisper-cheered.

'So what's the plan, Stan?' I asked.

No one answered. Hmm. Coming up with a plan might be the hard part. After much whispering, we decided this: we would use our most subtle and tactful sleuthing skills to find out what was going on. And we *would* find out. Or my name wasn't Nosy – I mean, Rosie – Parker.

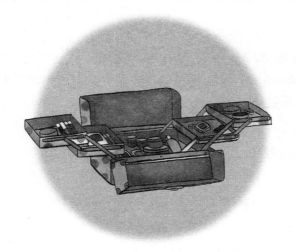

Chapter Five

Our cunning plan proved not to be so cunning after all. To be fair, going up to the twins and asking them about the whole argument-and-mother thing wasn't *that* subtle. But who would have thought the twins would react the way they did? They'd always been so friendly to us before. My horoscope for the day *had* said, 'Beware of a frank conversation.' Maybe I should start paying more attention to it.

'There's nothing wrong,' Paige said, turning away from Soph. 'Anyway, I'm needed on set now.'

'Argument? We never argue!' Shelby trilled when I asked her about it. 'Could you get me a glass of water, please?'

'We're *fine*,' they both said firmly to Abs as they walked off.

Hmm. We were stuck. I thought I'd have one last go and went in search of the twins. They were watching a run-through of the scene before theirs. It was a boring conversation between their 'mother' and 'father' in the bar of the hotel.

'Hi,' I whispered, carefully stepping over the cables and wires surrounding them. 'Look, we don't want to interfere, but we were just concerned, because like I said, I heard you arguing yesterday and –'

'Listen. This is none of your business,' Paige snapped, stepping back from me.

'Stop harassing us. If you and your friends don't leave us alone, we'll get you removed from this movie set for good,' Shelby said, threading her arm through Paige's. They both looked at me fiercely.

'Is everything all right here?' Misty asked,

suddenly appearing behind the twins. For once, I hadn't smelt her before I saw her.

'We're fine, thanks, Misty,' the girls chorused, smiling at her. 'Absolutely ripper.' But I saw Paige glance at me quickly – like, GET GONE!

'I'll be off then,' I said, scurrying away.

It was clear the twins didn't trust us. And they had every reason to be wary. After all, if your mother can betray you, so can three girls who are massivo fans and could easily sell your story to the papers. Celebs have to be careful who they confide in. We had to prove we were worth their trust before they'd let us help them. I called an emergency meeting in the make-up room.

'If only there was a way to show we can keep secrets, and we're completely cool,' said Abs, twirling her glasses in her hand.

'Well, it would help if you two were a bit more stylishly dressed,' Soph remarked, admiring her own flowery vest-and-blouse combo – 'just a little something I knocked up' (i.e. something only Soph could get away with).

'Oh, ha, ha. Not that kind of cool – the kind of people who are completely trustworthy because they know celebrities are just normal, really,' Abs explained.

'Yeah, but how do we do that?' I said, frustrated.

We sat there in silence for a while, staring at ourselves in the mirrors.

'Come on, Abs, think!' I said. 'You're the brainy one!'

'We could ignore the twins, I suppose,' said Soph. 'You know – they're always saying they're just ordinary. So we don't treat them differently – don't get them breakfast, just ignore them. That kind of thing.' She brushed some blusher on to her cheeks.

'Brilliant idea – except the whole point of us being here is to be helpful and do things like get them breakfast,' Abs pointed out.

I sighed. The only thing I could think of doing was to go up to them and say: WE CAN HELP YOU – OH, AND BY THE WAY, WE'RE

REALLY COOL, which obviously wasn't going to work. We would just have to hope they realised we were for real.

* * *

That afternoon, the twins went back to their swanky suite at the top of the hotel, because they weren't needed for the rest of the day. They looked really knackered, so Misty made them promise to go straight to sleep. I reckoned they needed to sort out their differences, not sleep. If only they'd confide in us!

Still, if I couldn't be a shoulder to cry on, at least I could still be a runner. Soph and Abs had been sent out to get pizza for the crew and wouldn't be back for ages. Penny suggested I help her by tidying the clothes in the twins' dressing room. She had to go and find butterfly hairclips, because Misty had suddenly demanded some for a scene the next day. The stars had told her the twins would benefit from wearing something to do with flying.

Anyway, as I walked across the hotel lobby, I was planning what I would say to Amanda Hawkins when we got back to school. I could get the twins to sign something that I could casually get out of my bag in front of Amanda, and then be all, 'Oh, yeah, Paige and Shelby, I wonder how they are. They said they'd call.' And Amanda would realise me and Abs and Soph were very cool and then she would stop commenting on every little thing I do in PE as if she's an Olympic athlete, which she so isn't.

I was just imagining her apologising to me for all the nasty things she's ever said, when suddenly a voice called, 'Rosie! Hey, Rosie Parker!'

I turned to see Mirage Mullins, the pop star!!! She looked amazing in a black catsuit and ankle boots, her blonde hair pushed back with a black headband. She ran across the lobby and hugged me, much to the amazement of her bodyguard and her PA, who stayed by her mountain of luggage.

'How've you been?' she laughed as we hugged. 'It's so good to see you.'

'You too, Mirage!' I said. It took me a second to get over feeling starstruck. So much for being completely cool and realising that stars were people too. Mirage was so down to earth, though, it seemed completely normal that a chart-topping superstar was hugging me.

'Hey, there's Mirage Mullins!' a voice said.

'With Rosie!' a très similar-sounding voice replied.

I looked behind Mirage to see the twins staring at us, their mouths hanging open. Mirage turned round too.

'G'day, Mirage!' said Paige, coming over. 'I'm Paige Sweetland. I'm a massive fan of yours.'

'And I'm Shelby,' Shelby said. 'Also a massive fan.'

'Nice to meet you,' Mirage said. 'And thanks. I love your soap, by the way.'

'They're making a film,' I said. '*Gemini*. Filming here in Hotel Londonia.'

'Ah, so that's why I can't get a room!' Mirage said.

'So how do *you* know Mirage?' Paige asked me.

The twins looked totally dumbfounded. *Ha!! You see? I'm not just good for getting coffees! I also hug mega-famous pop stars! Rosie Parker, friend and hugger of the stars, that's me.*

'Well –' I began.

'She's the secret of my success,' said Mirage, interrupting me. She grabbed my arm and led the way to some comfy sofas. 'Let's just say that Rosie and her friends helped me out of a huge hole last year. I really wouldn't be where I am today without them.' She squeezed my arm as we sat down.

I blushed. Paige and Shelby were staring at me. 'Did they?' said Paige. 'Wow.'

'Yup – I owe it all to them,' Mirage said. 'And I haven't seen them since.'

'Well, er, I've been busy at school –' I stammered.

'Oh, Rosie, I didn't mean it like that!' Mirage laughed. 'I've been a bit busy myself. I just meant I missed you lot!'

'Well, you two probably want to catch up,' said Shelby. 'We'll leave you to it. We were going for a walk anyway.'

'I thought you were going to sleep,' I said, without thinking. *Oops. That probably sounded really cheeky. They'll never talk to me now.*

'We don't have to do everything Misty tells us, do we?' Paige said, winking at me. 'Er, Rosie, could you come and talk to us later? In private? Suite sixteen, in about an hour?'

I nodded, amazed. They wanted to talk to me!!! This was good. This was better than good.

The twins said goodbye to Mirage, still looking a bit star-struck, which was really funny.

'They're nice,' Mirage said as they walked off.

'Yup. But they're in trouble,' I said. 'I just know it.'

'Ah, another mystery for the girls to solve! Well, with you and Abs and Soph on the case, you'll sort it out!' Mirage said.

I just hoped she was right.

Chapter Six

After a très fab catch-up with Mirage – with her PA hovering nervously nearby, trying to get her to leave because she had to rehearse for an awards ceremony – I got in the lift to go to the twins' suite. If you'd told me a few months ago that I would be going straight from chatting to Mirage Mullins to talk to the Sweetland twins, I would have told you to get a grip – now I was doing exactly that! I just wished the girls were with me to help. They'd be gutted they missed Mirage. I didn't have time to wait for them to come back. I couldn't be late for the twins – they'd never trust me again. I did text Abs:

> **Me:** Amazing!! Just bumped into Mirage! She sends luv.
> **Abs:** You lie!! What wearing?
> **Me:** Tell u l8r. Now going to see P&S – they want 2 talk!!!
> **Abs:** No way! B careful.

Abs was right. I had to make sure I didn't freak the twins out. And I had to get them to tell me everything about Misty and their mother. *And* I had to remember it all in my head so I could tell the girls. No pencil and paper this time, in case Misty found it and worked out I'd been talking to the twins. I definitely didn't trust her.

I felt really nervous as I knocked on the door of suite sixteen.

'Who is it?' said a voice.

'Er, Rosie,' I said.

'Oh, good. Come in.' Paige opened the door –

with a huge smile! Good start!

'Thanks for coming,' she said, ushering me into the most ENORMOUS hotel room I've ever seen. It had a really thick cream carpet and several sofas and a HUMONGOUS plasma-screen TV on one wall. The TV alone wouldn't fit into my lounge. And there were so many flowers! And candles! It was sooo beautiful.

Paige laughed at the look on my face. 'So you like our accommodation then?' she joked.

'This is only the sitting room,' Shelby said, leaping up from a sofa. 'Come and see one of the bedrooms.'

I followed the twins into one of several rooms that led off the main sitting room. Wow! There was a ginormous four-poster bed in the centre, and the bathroom had one of those baths that was sunk into the floor. I REALLY want one of those. When I am rich and famous, I will do all my important creative thinking in the bath. I'll have scented candles all around it and loads of bubble bath in it and it will be so relaxing and luxurious . . .

'Rosie?' Shelby said. 'Do you want a drink?' She opened the door of a cupboard that turned out to be a fridge! It was packed with soft drinks.

'A lemonade, please,' I said. It looked like they could probably spare one.

'Let's sit down,' Paige said, heading back into the sitting room. Shelby turned the TV off, which was a shame because *Hart Grove* was just about to start. They film it two months in advance, so that episode was old news to them. How weird would *that* be, to watch them on screen while sitting next to them?! Freaky.

'So,' I said, sitting down and acting all cool, 'what's the story, Rory?'

'Well, basically . . . what you said to us this morning was right,' Paige said. 'Shelby and I *did* have an argument yesterday. And it *was* about our mum.'

'Paige found a letter from her in Misty's handbag – which I *still* don't think she should have been going through – and it was addressed to us,' Shelby explained.

Quick, say something intelligent, Rosie! Impress them!

'Oh,' I said.

'I *told* you, I was looking for some aspirin!' Paige said, defensively. 'I only got a chance to read a bit of it, but it was really nice. She was saying she hadn't taken our money, and how much she missed us.'

'Well, of course she'd say that!' Shelby said.

'So why d'you think Misty had it in her bag?' I asked.

'Well, it was Misty who discovered Mum had been stealing from us. And she found all this evidence. Then, while we were still in shock, she told us she could see from our astrological charts that things would never run smoothly for us while Mum was in the picture,' Paige said.

'So she persuaded us to press for the divorce,' said Shelby, looking at her feet. 'I think she hid this letter from us so we wouldn't get upset. After all, she's right – things have been better since she became our guardian. We've got this movie, for a start, and she keeps us up to date with what's happening with our money.'

'Yeah, but we still don't really *see* any money. And we have to run everything past her. I feel like a five year old!' Paige complained.

'So, er, how come she became your guardian anyway?' I asked nervously. I had to hope this wasn't one question too far in the nosiness stakes. Still, they had said they wanted my help. And, as everyone who's ever watched a murder-mystery knows – Nan, for one – you have to find out all the facts before you can work out whodunit. Not that there'd been a murder. But there was a mystery. Oh, what the crusty old grandads was my brain going on about? *Listen, Rosie, listen!*

Paige was trying to answer the question. 'Well, she's been really supportive the whole time, ever since we met her – and things she said seemed to be right, you know. After all, we didn't have any money – what were we to think? All the stuff Misty said about Mum just seeing us as money-making machines made sense. I mean, we've been working since we were two! Misty seemed like the only person we could really trust. We had to have a guardian, since we're under age, and it felt right to have someone who could predict stuff. We don't really know many other people.' Paige looked a bit embarrassed.

'It must've been awful to divorce your mum though,' I said.

'Yeah, it was,' Shelby said, sniffing a bit. She looked like she was trying not to cry. 'She was so upset. But we were so sure she'd stolen from us.'

'And . . . you're not so sure now?' I asked, crossing my fingers and all my toes that I hadn't blown it.

'No,' said Paige firmly. 'Misty Van Deville is a complete fraud. I know that now. It said in mum's note that she's desperate for a reply to just one of the letters she's sent us, but we've never seen a single one until now. Misty's been keeping them from us. She can't see the future and she's definitely trying to push us around. I feel so stupid for believing her.'

'We both did,' Shelby whispered.

'I want to contact Mum,' Paige said. 'I think we

should get that letter, find out her new address and write to her – give her a chance to tell her side of the story.'

'We can't!' Shelby said. 'Misty will kill us! We promised not to let her into our lives again or things would go off course.'

'Look –' I began, then stopped because there was a soft 'thunk' outside the door. We all looked at each other.

'Someone's listening!' Paige whispered.

I leapt up and crept to the door. Then I flung it open and peered out. No one there. Although there was a très familiar perfume in the air . . .

Misty had been there – and she must have been listening!!!

Chapter Seven

When we got back to Penny's flat that night, I told the girls what had happened.

'So Misty knows they know she's a fraud,' Abs said.

'I wonder if she predicted *that*?' Soph snorted.

'The twins have got a problem. They wanted us to help them contact their mother. She had to sell the house and move after the divorce, and they don't know where she lives now. They wanted *us* to find her, so Misty wouldn't get suspicious of what they were doing,' I said.

'But now she's suspicious anyway,' Abs pointed out.

'Exactly. It's crucial that we get their mum's details as soon as possible.' I was impressed with myself. I sounded really determined and dynamic. The girls were hanging on my every word, so I hit them with my big idea. 'So I said we'd steal the letter from Misty's handbag.'

'What??' Abs cried.

'Well, OK, borrow it,' I said. 'It's addressed to the twins anyway, so it's not like Misty owns it.'

Soph's eyes had lit up. 'She always leaves her bag behind when she goes to talk to the director. I could grab it then! I'll hang around the dressing room all day tidying the clothes. She won't suspect a thing!'

'Good thinking, Batgirl,' I said, getting excited that we could actually do something to help Paige and Shelby. *And it's my plan! I am a tactical genius.*

'What are you lot scheming about?' Penny asked, poking her head round the door.

'Oh, we're going to ask the twins to sign a

photo of themselves for us,' Abs said quickly. 'You know, as a souvenir before we go.' That's what I love about Abs – she's so clever at thinking of stuff like that when it really matters. By the time I come up with a brilliant plan it's usually far too late.

'I'm sure they'd be very happy to do that,' Penny said. 'Now go to sleep!'

We snuggled down in our sleeping bags, wriggling with glee at the thought of helping Paige and Shelby. The next day was going to be sooo exciting!

* * *

Little did we know just *how* exciting the next day would actually be! When we got to the set, Paige wasn't in the twins' dressing room. Shelby was though, sitting on the sofa, fiddling with the tie of her dressing gown. Misty was standing near her, arms folded.

'Morning, Shelby!' I said cheerily, winking at her and giving her a thumbs-up to let her know we had a plan.

'G'day,' she said quietly.

Hmm. She didn't seem very pleased to see us. I looked closely at her and saw her eyes were a bit red. Maybe they'd had another argument.

'Where's Paige?' Penny asked.

'I don't know,' Shelby said, sounding really upset.

'It's very inconsiderate of her not to turn up this morning,' Misty said sharply.

'She's never done this before. I don't understand what's happened –' Shelby began.

'Well, we must be professional!' Misty interrupted. 'We can't hold filming up. You can do her scenes for her, Shelby. No one will realise you're not her. We'll add a mole on your forehead with make-up. That way we won't waste a day of everyone's time, not to mention their money.'

Shelby nodded miserably. Me, Soph and Abs looked at each other. This was seriously weird. Where was Paige?

'Just the two raisin bagels this morning, then,' Misty said in our general direction. 'And get the make-up artist to come in here pronto.'

'Yes, Misty,' we chorused and ran off.

'I smell a rat,' Abs said.

'Me too,' Soph said. 'Why hasn't Paige turned up this morning?'

'And why isn't Misty more worried?' I said.

'Yeah – after all, she needs Paige to earn her money!' Abs pointed out.

'Maybe she saw in the stars that this would happen, and she knows Paige will turn up eventually,' Soph said sarcastically.

'Let's talk to Shelby later,' I suggested. 'She might have some idea where Paige is.' I gasped. 'Maybe she's gone to find their mum!'

But when we went to find Shelby a few hours later, Melissa and Felipe were in the dressing room, and it was really difficult to ask her anything. Then Misty came in and frowned at us. It was obvious we were hovering about, waiting to talk to Shelby, and she wasn't happy at all. Especially with Abs coughing and spluttering the whole time she was there.

'Let's come back later,' I whispered.

So we left and went next door, to the empty dressing room. Soph peeked out of the door to see when Misty left again. While we were waiting, we compiled a list.

Five things we definitely know:

1. Paige is missing, which is seriously worrying, considering even her *twin* doesn't seem to know where she is.
2. Misty has kept a letter from the twins' mum in her handbag and hasn't told them about it. Très dodgy.
3. Misty is very controlling and interfering. And rich, seeing as she can spend so much on perfume and posh clothes and dodgy earrings.
4. Shelby is scared of Misty.
5. We have to do something about it!

'OK, she's gone, and so have the others,' Soph whispered after about quarter of an hour.

'Quick!' I said, tiptoeing to the door.

We ran like lightning to Shelby's door and rushed in without knocking.

'What are you doing here?' she asked, startled. 'You've got to go!'

'We want to know what's going on,' I said. 'Where's Paige?'

'I don't know!' she wailed.

'Did you see her this morning? Did she say anything to you?' Abs demanded.

'Look, you've got to go. Please leave,' Shelby begged, pacing up and down the room. 'Misty will be back soon.'

'That's why you have to tell us what you know *now*,' I said, grabbing Shelby's hands and forcing her stop pacing.

Her eyes darted about the room and she pulled free of me. 'Please, just go!' she said again. 'All of you. Just leave it alone.'

She was really scared and didn't seem to know anything. We had to give up.

'Come on, girls,' Abs said. 'Let's go.'

We trooped out of the dressing room, and came face to face with – Penny!

'Oh, Penny, you scared us!' Soph said.

'What are you up to, girls?' Penny demanded, hands on her hips. She looked really angry. 'Misty has complained to me that you're being a nuisance. If you don't behave, I'll have no choice but to leave you at home from now on. Understand?'

'Yes, Penny,' we muttered.

'OK, if you could help wind some cabling in the ballroom, that would be very useful.'

'Yes, Penny,' we said.

As soon as we were out of earshot, Soph said, 'Oooh, that Misty. Complaining about us – I ask you! The cheek of it! We've been nothing but helpful all week.'

'I bet she's got something to do with Paige's disappearance,' I said.

'D'you think?' Soph said.

'She's being bizarrely calm about it all. I bet most people who work for a celeb would go bonkers if they went missing!'

'Especially if her twin didn't know where she was,' Abs pointed out. 'Yeah, I think you're right. Misty knows something about it – and she's scared we'll find out.'

'So what shall we do? We can't let her scare us off!' Soph said.

'I dunno. But she can only tell us what to do while we're on the set,' Abs said.

'Yeah, we need to get away from here,' I said, following Abs's train of thought. 'So let's follow her tonight and see where she goes! I bet we'll find some clues.'

'OK,' the others agreed. 'But we'd better be careful.'

'And how will we get round Penny?' I asked.

* * *

'So we thought we'd make the most of being in London and go to the huge cinema in Leicester Square where all the premières take place,' Abs was saying to Penny. Abs is so great. She always has a plan.

Soph and I nodded behind her, totally innocent.

'Good idea,' Penny said. 'I suppose it's boring for you to spend all your spare time in my little flat. Now, you know how to get back, don't you?'

'Yup,' we chorused. 'Piccadilly line.'

'Well have fun! Tell me what the film's like. I've read good reviews.' Penny hugged us and then rushed off in the direction of the dressing rooms again. Luckily she was too preoccupied with Misty's latest demands to notice us high-fiving each other behind her.

That afternoon, instead of going to the cinema, we stationed ourselves in the lobby of the hotel. Filming had finished for the day, so it was only a matter of time before Misty would come through the lobby to go – well, wherever she had to go. We'd taken the precaution of sitting separately, with our backs to the direction she'd be coming from.

'I'm really worried she'll walk past and we won't see her,' I said, biting my nails. This subterfuge was stressful.

'Sssh. Check your mirror,' Abs hissed. She'd had an amazing idea, as usual. Even though we weren't facing the right way, we could see the lobby by looking in mirrors she'd borrowed from the make-up room earlier. It did make sense to avoid making eye contact with Misty, anyway (and Penny, if she happened to walk past). I just wasn't sure it was going to work, especially since Soph was seriously distracted by her own reflection.

'D'you think I'd look better with a fringe?' she asked.

'Well, it would depend on what you were wearing,' I said reluctantly, knowing this would start Soph off on a fashion daydream.

'You're right. So, if I wore that hooded dress I saw in *Vogue* –'

Suddenly, Abs stood up. 'Quick!' she hissed. 'She's going outside!'

Soph and I leapt up and we all scurried to the revolving door of the hotel. We could see Misty walking down the street to the left.

'Come on!' Soph said. 'Let's go!'

So we followed her. She hadn't gone very far before she went into another hotel.

'I thought she was staying at the Londonia?' I said.

'She is,' Abs replied.

'So why's she going in there?' Soph asked.

'Let's find out!' I said.

We followed her into the lobby of the hotel and stood behind a humongous pot plant near the bar.

'Good evening, Madam,' the receptionist said to Misty.

'Good evening. The keys to room three two five please,' she replied.

'Certainly, Miss Stoker. Will you be requiring anything else?' the man inquired.

'No thank you. Oh – actually, please see to it that I am not disturbed.'

'Certainly, Madam.'

Abs, Soph and I looked at each other. 'Miss *Stoker*???' mouthed Soph. We shrugged. Misty Van Deville was definitely up to something!!

Suddenly, Abs squeaked and grabbed us. She

was heading our way! We turned frantically and spotted a door behind us. Diving through it, we pulled the door shut just as Misty went into the bar.

'D'you think she saw us?' Abs panted.

'Ssssh,' I whispered, waiting for the door handle to start to turn.

But it didn't happen, so after a minute we relaxed and looked about us. We were in the hotel's laundry room. It was filled with uniforms and sheets and towels, all piled up on shelves around the room.

'So what's the plan, Stan?' I asked.

Chapter Eight

What *was* the plan? We all looked at each other, stumped.

'She must be hiding something here. In room three two five,' Abs said, looking at a piece of paper where she'd scribbled Misty's fake name and the room number.

'Maybe the letter,' Soph said. 'I looked in her handbag today and I couldn't see it.'

'But why would she hire a room in a different hotel, just for that?' I asked. 'Hmm. We need Nan. She'd have some ideas of what Misty could be up to. Or she'd know what Jessica Fletcher would do, anyway.'

'*I* know what Jessica Fletcher would do,' Abs said suddenly. 'Look.' She pointed to the freshly laundered maids' uniforms hanging up behind us. 'She would go and investigate. And we have the perfect disguise!'

'You want me to wear *that*?' Soph asked, disgusted.

'Look, if J-Lo can wear a maid's outfit in *Maid in Manhattan* and still look totally funky, then we can too!' I said.

'We haven't got time for this. Come on – while Misty's in the bar, we should go to her room and try to investigate,' Abs said.

Ten minutes later, we were in the service lift, trying to look professional, like normal maids. Luckily, we'd spent the whole week trying to look like we knew what we were doing and running around a hotel, so it didn't feel that strange.

'How are we going to get in?' whispered Soph to Abs.

'I don't know. Maybe we can find another maid and borrow her keys or something,' Abs said lamely. 'Sacré bleu! I can't think of everything!'

'Well, let's knock on the door first at least,' I suggested. 'If there's someone in there, we could pretend we've got the wrong room.'

We arrived at the third floor and found room 325. I took a deep breath.

'Room service!' I called, and banged on the door.

The door opened a tiny crack and a man poked his head out.

'Yes?' he said. He didn't look very happy at being disturbed.

'Er, hello. Just wondering if you wanted any room service?' I asked.

'No,' he said.

'And, er, are there any dirty plates we can collect?' Abs said, trying to see past him.

He sighed and turned round to check. As he did so, the door opened a bit wider and we could see more of the room. And in it was Paige – gagged and bound to a chair!!!

We all gasped and the man snapped his head back to us. 'No, there aren't – now go away!' he said gruffly, slamming the door.

'He's got Paige!' Soph whispered, urgently, jumping up and down.

Just then, we saw one of the real maids approaching with a trolley.

'I know! Quick, hide!' Abs said, running down the corridor.

When we were back in the lift, we all gasped again.

'I can't believe Paige is tied up!' I said.

'I *knew* there was something fishy about that woman!' Soph said. 'And who's he?'

'What are we going to do?' Abs said.

'We have to rescue her!' I said.

'Yeah!' Soph said.

'Without running into Misty,' Abs said.

'Let's hide in the laundry room again,' Soph suggested. 'We can watch the lobby and the bar from there and see when the coast is clear.'

We sat in the laundry room for an hour, hoping

no one would come in. We took it in turns to peek out of the door. It seemed like we'd spent all day peeking in or out of rooms.

'I quite like this outfit actually,' Soph said after a while. 'It has that sense of old-fashioned style that is very in at the moment. Look at the sleeves.'

'Yes, because we *are* on fashion parade,' I said.

'You laugh now, but you'll all be wearing puffed sleeves in six months,' Soph said.

I winced. 'Really?'

'Sssh!' said Abs, at the door. 'I can see Misty! She's with the man from the room!'

We leapt up and tried to look out too.

'Stop pushing! You'll make me fall out!' Abs said. 'OK, they've handed their keys in! They're going towards the door . . . Yes, they've gone! Now!'

We sauntered casually out of the laundry room, trying to look like we'd just been arranging towels. It was time to put our plan into action. Soph went to call the lift, pushing a trolley that held a laundry bag containing our real clothes. Abs and I went to reception. There was only one person behind the desk, a girl.

'Hello,' Abs said to her. 'I'm a new maid, and I've lost my map of the hotel.' This was Abs's genius trick. If it worked.

The girl just looked at her. We both beamed at her encouragingly.

'You couldn't get me a replacement map, could you? I'd be very grateful.'

I was impressed by Abs's acting. She was totally a confused maid.

'OK, I'll get you another one,' the girl sighed. 'But don't lose this one too.' She went into the back room behind reception. *And the award goes to Abigail Flynn!*

I spotted my chance and leaned over the desk to snag the keys to room 325. I headed for the lift, Abs following me with her replacement map.

'Quick! Third floor!' she said to Soph.

'Good acting, Abs,' I said admiringly. 'Mr Lord would be proud of you!'

'Thanks,' Abs said, smoothing her hair. 'And you were very quick at getting the keys, Rosie.'

'I missed it! Your starring moment!' Soph complained.

'We'll re-enact it for you later,' Abs reassured her. 'Right now we've got to focus on rescuing Paige. We don't know when Misty and the man will come back!'

When we got to room 325, it took ages to open the door, but we managed at last. We ran to Paige, whose eyes were huge at the sight of us. Soph removed her gag.

'Oh, am I ever glad to see you guys!' Paige gasped. 'Ow!'

'Sorry,' I said, struggling with the ropes that bound her to the chair.

'I can't believe she tied you up and got a horrible man to watch over you!' Soph said.

'That man is my father!' Paige said. 'He and Misty are working together to steal our money!'

'You lie!!' I said. 'Your *father*?'

'I know,' Paige said. 'Well, he says he's my father anyway. I've never seen a photo of him cos mum destroyed them all when he walked out on us, so I'm not really sure. If he is our dad, we're definitely better off without him!'

'We *knew* Misty was up to something!' Abs said, helping me with the ropes.

'They've gone out, but we don't know when they'll be back,' Soph said, checking the time.

'They've gone for dinner,' Paige said. 'I heard Misty complaining about how bad the food is at Hotel Londonia.'

'I'm not surprised. All she eats is those raisin bagels!' Soph said.

'And voilà! Freedom at last!' I said, as Paige struggled up from the chair.

'Thanks, girls!' she said, hugging us.

'No problemo,' I said, grinning hugely. We'd done it!

'Right – let's go!' Abs said.

'Don't you want your mum's letter?' asked Soph. 'It wasn't in Misty's handbag earlier, but it might be here.'

'Good idea. Let's look for it, and anything else to prove what Misty's been up to,' said Paige.

'OK, but let's be quick. They may change their minds and come back!' Abs warned.

We all ran to a different bit of the room and began searching.

'Shelby's really worried about you,' I told Paige.

'They took me from our suite while I was asleep last night. I woke up here this morning, tied up!' Paige explained, hunting through a suitcase. 'It was terrifying. Ah! Look, here are some bank statements.' She held up a sheaf of papers.

'And I've found a laptop. I bet it's got some incriminating stuff on it,' Abs said.

'D'you think we should take the laptop though?' I said nervously. 'Wouldn't that be stealing?'

'Well, yeah, I guess,' Abs said slowly.

'Look, they kidnapped me, which is worse, so *I'll* take the laptop,' Paige said. 'It's only to get evidence anyway, not to keep.'

'Oooh, look!' Sophie said, waving an envelope. 'Here's the letter from your mum in Misty's *other* handbag!'

I looked at my watch. 'We've been ages. We'd better go. Come with us to Penny's flat, Paige. You can't go back to the hotel tonight.'

'Yeah, OK. But let me call Shelby to let her know I'm safe,' Paige said, bundling everything into a bag and throwing a dressing gown over her pyjamas.

'You can use my mobile,' Soph offered. 'But not till we're out of here!'

We peeked out of the door. No one in sight.

'Better not use the lift in case Misty's in the lobby,' Abs said, grabbing the bag with our clothes in it.

'And my dad,' Paige said, shivering. 'Some reunion that was.'

'Let's go down the stairs. Hotels always have stairs,' I said, borrowing Abs's map. 'Here, look.' I led them down the corridor.

We legged it down the stairs and ran through a fire-escape door by the kitchens that led out into an alley.

'Hey!' came a shout from behind us, but we ran

on, until we turned a corner and were on a main road.

'Phew!' said Soph. 'Come on. Let's go back and talk to Penny. She'll know what to do. Here's my phone, Paige.'

'Thanks,' Paige said, dialling as we hurried to the nearest tube station, keeping an eye out for Misty and Paige's dad.

'Shelby? It's me!' Paige said. 'Yeah, I'm fine . . . Honestly. I'm fine.' She started sniffing and crying. 'I know, I know. Listen – don't let Misty or anyone else come and get you, OK? She and someone claiming to be our dad kidnapped me! . . . Yeah. Look, when she finds I'm gone, she'll know we're on to her. So don't talk to her!! . . . We're going to sort it out . . . me, Rosie, Abs and Soph . . . Yeah, I know! They're great. OK. Speak to you in a bit. We're going to Penny's flat now.'

Paige stopped and handed Soph's phone back to her, wiping her eyes.

I rummaged in the pocket of my maid's uniform and found a tissue for her.

'Thanks,' she said in a wobbly voice. 'And thanks for rescuing me. You girls are the best!'

Chapter Nine

When we got to Penny's flat she was amazed to see Paige.

'Hello, Paige,' she said. 'What are you doing here? And why are you wearing your pyjamas?'

'I was kidnapped –' she replied breathlessly.

'And we found her!' I said.

'It was Misty!' Soph shouted.

'And Paige's dad,' Abs said.

'These girls rescued me!' Paige said proudly.

'Hold on, hold on,' said Penny, looking very confused. 'Sit down and tell me what happened.'

As we all talked frantically, Penny held up her hands. 'One at a time, *please*!'

'Abs, *you* tell her,' I said.

As Abs talked, Penny looked more and more horrified. 'She tied you up, Paige? But why?'

'I was on to her. I suppose she thought she could scare me into going along with it,' Paige said.

'I can't believe it. I thought she was a bit strange, but that's criminal! We must tell the police.' Penny gave Paige a hug. 'You poor thing. You must have been terrified! I'm so glad you're OK.'

Paige smiled. 'Thank goodness for these three!' she said, looking at us gratefully.

We beamed in response.

'Yes, you three. What on earth did you think you were doing, following Misty, and stealing keys and a laptop? You could have got into serious trouble!' Penny said sternly.

'Yeah, but Paige –' Soph began.

'But nothing,' Penny said. 'Next time, tell me

first before you decide to go off on your own.'

'Yes, Penny,' we said, looking a bit sheepish.

'But since you *did* do all that, well done,' she said, smiling at us. 'That was some good detective work.'

'Nan would be proud of me,' I said, grinning. I had a strange craving for a custard cream.

It was so cool that Paige was safe – now we just had to make sure Shelby would be too.

* * *

Half an hour later, two police officers were enjoying a cup of tea in Penny's lounge and writing down everything we were saying.

'So you, er, *borrowed* those uniforms then?' the male officer said, looking at the outfits me, Abs and Soph were still wearing.

'Er, yes. We didn't have time to take them back, but we will, won't we?' I said earnestly, looking at the other two.

Abs nodded, but Soph hesitated.

'Soph?' I said sternly.

'Yeah, all right,' she muttered.

'Um, I don't want to interrupt, but I'm really worried about my sister, officers,' Paige said. Talk about acting skills – she could turn on the charm. She managed to sound respectful and earnest, while clearly feeling they were slow-witted fools. She'd been fidgeting like crazy while the three of us told our story. 'When Misty finds I'm gone, she'll go straight to our room in Hotel Londonia. And heaven only knows what she'll do to Shelby. When I spoke to Shelby earlier, she was really scared.'

'No need to worry, miss,' the woman police officer said kindly. 'We've already sent some colleagues round to talk to your sister, and to make sure your – er, *astrologer* doesn't come near her. In fact, they will arrest her if they see her.'

'Oh, good.' Paige sat back, relieved.

'And what about the man – I mean, Paige and Shelby's dad?' I asked.

'They've been told to look out for him too,' the police officer replied. 'No need to worry about

Shelby. Now, let's go over it again, Miss Sweetland. Tell us everything you remember hearing your kidnappers say. And then . . . um . . . perhaps you wouldn't mind signing an autograph for my daughter? She's a huge fan.'

'Sure,' said Paige, sipping her tea, calm now.

Abs, Soph and I looked at each other. It had been a long day, but a good one. After all, how often do you rescue a kidnapped film star from her deranged astrologer?

* * *

The next day, we all went to the set together. Paige had stayed over, sleeping on the sofa, and Soph was très proud that Paige was wearing some of her clothes. Paige was forced to, because she only had her pyjamas – but still, she'd chosen *Soph's* clothes, and that meant a lot to Soph.

When we walked into the hotel lobby, Shelby rushed over and hugged Paige. Then she hugged all of us. Then she hugged Paige again.

'I'm sorry I didn't believe you,' she said to

Paige. 'I've been such an idiot. I was really worried about you yesterday. Misty made me do all of your scenes too. I'm so sorry.'

'Don't be silly,' Paige smiled. 'I'm just so glad these three found me.'

Shelby turned to us. 'Thanks so much, girls. I'm sorry I was rude to you. I was just so scared.'

'No problemo,' Abs said. 'The main thing is you're both fine.'

'Oh, and guess what, Shelby?' Paige said. 'I got Mum's number off her letter and had a long chat with her last night. She's flying over!'

Shelby burst into tears. 'Oh, thank goodness!' They had another long hug.

'She's been writing to us every week, she told me, but I guess Misty found the letters before we did,' Paige said.

'I feel so bad about how we treated her,' Shelby said.

'Look, you weren't to know Misty had set her up,' I said. 'It's perfectly understandable. Why wouldn't you believe what Misty told you? After all, you've been famous since you were tiny, and we all know what *that* does to people . . .' I trailed off, aware that everyone was staring at me. I had just basically called the twins weirdos. Ooops. Foot in mouth again.

'Yeah, well, anyway, the show must go on!' said Paige. 'What's the schedule for the day?'

At that point Felipe, Melissa and Robert rushed up to Paige.

'Paige, baby!' Felipe wailed, sweeping her into a bear hug. 'What stress you have suffered! What terrible, terrible things! I cannot believe that woman tied you up! Let me look at you!'

Paige looked a bit bemused as Felipe held her at arm's length, then hugged her again while Melissa stroked one of her hands with tears in her eyes.

'Paige, darling, we're so glad you're safe,' Robert boomed, patting her on the back. 'Shelby did very well yesterday but it's better to have both girls on set, eh? Ha, ha!'

'Thank you. Anyway, I'm fine now and ready to start shooting,' Paige said, sitting down on one of the sofas in the lobby in an attempt to get away from everyone who was stroking her.

'Ah yes, darling. Very professional of you,' Robert said. 'But when we heard from Shelby what had happened, I realised you wouldn't be able to work today. And the police have told me they think Miss Van Deville might arrive here at some point. I couldn't possibly shoot in such circumstances, with the danger of being interrupted by the boys in blue at any moment! So we are all having a day off filming. Hang the cost! I have ordered everyone to relax, to enjoy London's wonderful parks, and to take care of themselves.'

Me, Abs and Soph grinned at each other. A day without taking messages from one end of the hotel to the other! A day without tripping over cables! A day without seeing Paige and Shelby! Oh. Not so good.

'Come on, girls,' Penny said. 'I think we all need to have a celebratory drink. Who's for milkshakes and ice cream?'

'Me!' said Soph.

'Me!' said Abs.

'Me!' I echoed.

'Us too,' Shelby and Paige said. 'But we'll see you there. We just want to sort out one thing . . .'

So the four of us went to the diner on the corner and ordered the most chocolatey, over-the-top ice creams they had.

'I still can't believe you dressed up as maids,' Penny said, slurping her ice cream.

'You mock, but just you wait,' Soph said, pointing at Penny with her dripping spoon. 'In six months, those outfits will be in *Vogue*.'

'Right,' Penny said.

'Really. In fact –' Soph began.

'Hi, everyone,' Shelby said as she and Paige came up to our table. 'We've got some news.'

'We've just been talking to Robert,' Paige said, 'and we persuaded him there would be no movie without you three. If you hadn't found me . . . well, who knows what might have happened. He owes you everything. So he's agreed to let you be extras in the next scene!'

'WHAT??!' Me, Soph and Abs all screamed.

'You're going to be in *Gemini*!' Paige and Shelby cried.

I'M GOING TO BE A MOVIE ACTRESS!!!

* * *

We spent the whole of that day just chilling with Paige and Shelby. It was coolissimo. They normally can't do very much when they're in a foreign city, because they're so busy filming and giving interviews, and because they're so recognisable and they get chased by paparazzi. But when we went out shopping with them, no one really looked at us. We were just a big group of girls, who giggled A LOT. It was great.

That night it took us AGES to get to sleep because we were so excited about being in the film. We were only going to be in a crowd scene, but the twins had promised us we'd be at the front, and we'd definitely see ourselves in the final thing. It was sooo exciting!!!

When I woke up the next day, I had an enormous spot on my chin. Oh, joy. What perfect timing. And when we got to the set, we still had to get everyone's breakfasts, but then we were ushered into the make-up room and Melissa did our make-up (she had to spend ages covering my spot). It was fabissimo – I could so get used to the pampering involved in being a celeb. Then Penny gave us some cool clothes to wear, and suddenly we were being shouted at by the director.

'No, don't look at the camera, look here! At the twins! Everybody!'

We had to be hotel guests, applauding the twins as they walked through the ballroom, which was filled with guests. Simple, you'd think. But oh, no. Mr Slavedriver Director made us do it about fifty times! He was worse than our drama teacher, Mr Lord. Really, what did it matter if I looked down at one point? I thought I'd caught my heel in something. It would have been worse if I'd fallen flat on my face. Now *that* would have been worth shouting about.

Anyway, we finally wrapped the scene – check out my insider knowledge of movie lingo – and me, Soph and Abs flopped, exhausted, into armchairs.

'I never thought filming would be so tiring,' Abs said.

'I know,' Soph agreed. 'My feet are killing me!' She stuck out her legs, admiring the killer black stilettos she'd insisted on wearing, despite Penny's protests.

'Oi, you!' came a shout from behind a camera. 'We need a new light bulb here – go and get one, would you?'

I sighed and got up. Everything was back to normal.

Just then, Paige and Shelby rushed up.

'Where are you going, Rosie?' Paige said. 'You have to hear this!' She grabbed my hand, forcing me to sit down again.

'They've caught Misty and our dad!' Shelby said. 'They were at the airport, trying to get back to Australia.'

'Wow!' we all said.

'They obviously realised the game was up when I escaped,' Paige said. 'They're in police custody now.'

'Misty's moon must have been in Jupiter. She always says that when things go wrong for her!' Shelby laughed.

We all laughed, totally relieved. It was so good to know Misty wasn't going to reappear on the set, ordering everyone about and reeking of her yucky perfume.

'Paige? Shelby?' a voice said.

We turned to see a short, dark-haired woman standing in the doorway of the ballroom.

'Mum!' the twins both said, and ran to her, hugging her tightly.

Me, Soph and Abs looked at each other.

'Light bulb?' I said, and we crept away, leaving the twins and their mother to catch up. After all, they had a lot to say to each other.

Chapter Ten

So *obviously* that was our most exciting Easter holiday ever! It was sooo cool telling everyone at school how we'd spent the past two weeks.

'Yeah, right, like the Sweetland twins would hang around with you lot,' said Amanda Hawkins, catty as ever, when she heard our news. Her cronies, Lara Neils and Keira Roberts, sniggered.

'Actually –' I began, outraged.

'We don't have to prove ourselves to you,' Abs said, interrupting me. I was a bit annoyed she'd interrupted, because I was all set to make a cutting remark, but then she winked. *Ah, she has a plan.*

'Spoken like a true liar,' Amanda sneered. 'Here's a message for you three saddos: don't bother to invent stuff to make your pathetic lives sound more exciting. We're not interested.'

'OK, Amanda, whatever you say,' Abs said cheerily. Then she casually pushed up her sleeve, to reveal a silver charm bracelet EXACTLY like the ones the twins were famous for wearing.

Amanda's mouth dropped open. Abs nudged me and Soph and we both pushed up our sleeves too, to reveal matching bracelets.

'Bye!' we called, waving our arms in unison so the bracelets jangled as we walked off.

Amanda was still staring at us in disbelief as we turned a corner. Then we collapsed into giggles.

'Abs, you are brilliant!' I said admiringly.

'Did you see her face?!' Soph said, holding her sides, she was laughing so much.

Abs flicked her hair back and grinned. 'Well, she had it coming,' she said.

'It was so nice of the twins to get us these,'

I said, jangling the charms on my bracelet for, like, the millionth time. 'I just love the way that mine has a Sagittarius sign on it.'

'My Pisces one is much nicer though,' Soph said, admiring hers.

'What are you girls doing here? Shouldn't you be getting to class?' boomed a voice.

We turned round. It was Mr Lord.

'We were just admiring our presents from Paige and Shelby Sweetland, sir,' Soph said sweetly. 'You know, after we were runners on that film set this holiday.'

'Runners, eh?' Mr Lord said. 'When I was in *Doctor Who*, we didn't have runners. I had to get my own coffee. Have I told you about the time I was a Cyberman?'

'Yes, you have,' I said quickly. 'Oh, gosh, we'd better get to our English class. Bye, sir.'

We hurried away, leaving Mr Lord muttering, '*Runners*. I don't know . . .'

It took a while to settle back into normal life after all the excitement. Then, a few months later, we got a call from Penny saying we were invited to the world première of *Gemini*! Paige and Shelby had got us invites since we were 'crucial to its success', and they had told everyone. Since the film was set and filmed in London, the première was going to be in London, too, so this meant we were going to be some of the first people to see it! And we'd be seeing ourselves on screen for the first time. It was TRÈS nerve-racking. I just knew the spot on my chin was going to be the biggest thing on the screen, and my hair would look like a bird's nest, even though Felipe had spent ages making sure it looked nice.

'Stop fidgeting, Rosie!' Penny demanded. She was on her knees, fixing the hem of my dress. We were in her flat getting ready for the big night, and my stomach kept scrunching up every time I thought about that red carpet. We'd be walking along in front of all those cameras! I was bound to trip up, blinded by all the flashes. Or close my eyes in a photo, or do something else really stupid.

'You look amazing, Rosie,' Abs said. She was already dressed – Penny was leaving Soph till last.

'So do you,' I said. Abs was wearing a black dress that was all sparkly. It fitted her perfectly and she looked très elegant. Penny was so clever! I smoothed my deep blue dress over my hips. Even though I was nervous, I was pretty pleased with the outfit, which matched my eyes. It was a shame Penny had just borrowed the dresses.

'I'm so proud of you girls,' Penny said, trying to grin with pins in her mouth.

We smiled. Just then, there was a yell from the bathroom. 'Penny! I think I've cracked it!' shouted Soph.

'Oh, dear,' Penny said.

Soph threw open the bathroom door and stalked dramatically into the room.

'Your hair!' we all screeched. She'd only gone and chopped herself a fringe – very badly! With all her curls bobbing about around her face, it looked extra-awful.

'What will Felipe say?' Penny said as she gazed at Soph, who was looking all pleased with herself.

'Oh, Felipe is lovely, but he doesn't do *funky* hair,' Soph said, waving her hand dismissively. 'This haircut will go with the cool sixties look I'm working tonight.' She pointed at the outfit she'd already put on – a black-and-white mini-dress with white boots that went over her knees.

Penny laughed. 'Well, I have to hand it to you, Soph. You always do things differently. I just hope other people won't start doing the same, or I'll be out of a job!'

'The masses will always need your guidance, Penny,' Soph said generously, plonking herself on the sofa to do her eyeliner. 'Just look at these two.'

'Oi!' me and Abs said.

'What?' Soph looked up at us. 'I'm saying you look gorgeous now.'

'*Now*?' I said.

'Yeah. Penny's amazing, isn't she?' she said.

Abs and I looked at each other and burst out laughing. 'Yep, she is,' we agreed. 'She really is.'

When we got to Leicester Square, I couldn't believe how many people were there! There were barriers up to prevent everyone going on the special red carpet, and the place was packed. They were all waiting to catch a glimpse of the Sweetland twins. Our car stopped at the end of the red carpet.

'Follow me, girls,' Penny said, getting out.

We scrambled out after her and nervously stood there for a moment.

'Come on!' Penny started to walk up towards the cinema doors. They suddenly looked very far away. There were loads of people shouting and I froze. I couldn't think, let alone move. Everyone would be staring, and pointing, and criticising my outfit. Let's face it, that's what I mostly buy *Star Secrets* for — to pore over photos of actresses in outrageous dresses and rate them out of ten (and argue with Soph about them). The pressure!

'Coming, Rosie?' Abs said, turning round. She and Soph had already started after Penny. 'You've got to get out of the way for the next car!'

'Oh, yeah,' I said, coming back to life and starting to walk up the red carpet. (Now there's a sentence I never thought I'd say!)

It was a bit disappointing though, in the end. I could hear people saying, 'Who are they?' as we walked past. And the photographers took a few snaps and then stopped as they realised we were nobodies. But there were other people on the carpet too now – we waved at Melissa – and it was sooo cool to be on this side of the barrier for once with all the D-list celebs! I couldn't believe how many *Big Brother* contestants and other reality-TV stars there were, posing for photos and stopping to chat with the people behind the barriers.

We didn't really have anything to do because we're not famous, so we just hung about. But then, after a while, we were ushered into the cinema. The seats were labelled so we knew where to sit. We saw Paige and Shelby arrive last and go right to the front row. They looked amazing – they were wearing matching oyster-coloured gowns. Très elegant!

Robert gave a little intro and then the film began. It was really good – so funny, and the twins were brilliant!!! It was so weird that scenes I'd watched being filmed were on the big screen. They made sense now! I was seriously impressed by how good it all looked.

However, if you'd blinked, you would have missed us, our scene was over so fast. Even though I was waiting for it, I almost forgot to look for us. I thought I saw me briefly (no spot – thank you, Melissa!), and Soph's elbow . . . Oh, well, I'd just have to buy the DVD and freeze-frame it!

When it had finished, the credits rolled and everyone stayed in their seats to watch them. I guess if you're in it, you want to see your name! Anyway, just as we were getting fidgety, right at the end, suddenly this flashed up on the screen:

A HUGE THANK YOU TO ROSIE, SOPHIE AND ABIGAIL, WITHOUT WHOM THIS FILM WOULD NOT HAVE BEEN FINISHED.

Can you believe it? We were still reeling with shock when, suddenly, a spotlight came on over our heads. As we blinked in the brightness, Paige and Shelby stood up and shouted, 'There they are!'

Everyone turned to look. And then they all stood up and clapped us. Yes, we got a standing ovation!! From celebrities!!! We didn't know what to do other than grin like idiots. Which we did – a lot.

Then Paige and Shelby came up the aisle to where we were sitting and gave us a humongous bouquet of flowers each.

'Thanks so much,' Paige said in my ear as we hugged.

I couldn't stop grinning. 'Pleasure!' I said.

'See you at the party!' Shelby said.

* * *

SACRÉ BLEU!!! The party was AMAZING. They held it in this club, and Penny said we could only go if we didn't drink, and when we got in there, they'd made loads of non-alcoholic cock-tails for the twins and us. My first one had three pieces of fruit and an umbrella in it! It was brilliant just standing there watching everyone chatting and dancing. Actually, watching people dancing was the best bit, because – well, let's just say that some reality-TV celebrities think they can dance, but I've seen budgies with better moves than theirs.

It was great being with all the crew again. Most of them remembered us. Robert came and hugged us and said, 'Marvellous to see you, marvellous,' and then moved on to the next group of people. And Paige and Shelby were in huge demand, of course, so we didn't get long to talk to them. But it was just brilliant, feeling part of this team and celebrating the end of a project we'd all worked on together.

At midnight, Penny rounded us up to go home. I confess I was yawning a lot by then. It's tiring partying with celebrities, you know. In the taxi home, we made this list:

**Top five reasons why working on this film
was great:**

1. We got to party with loads of celebs.
2. We got to bring a family back together.
3. We got to meet Paige and Shelby.
4. We got to walk up a red carpet . . .
5. We got to be film stars ourselves!!!!!!!!!!

As I flopped into bed, I thanked my lucky stars
that the three of us have a talent for trouble!

Fact File

NAME: Abs (Abigail) Flynn

AGE: 14

STAR SIGN: Libra

HAIR: Long brown bob

EYES: Green

LOVES: Hanging out with Rosie and Soph and solving mysteries

HATES: Beetroot and babysitting her little sister, Megan

LAST SEEN: Tucking into a burger at Trotters with Rosie and Soph

MOST LIKELY TO SAY: 'Don't stress – I'll help!'

WORST CRINGE EVER: Accidentally sitting on a boy's lap in the cinema when she came back from the loo. Oh, the shame!

CRACK THE CODE

Be like Mirage and use this cool code to send your secret messages

WHAT TO DO:

Each letter has a number so, when you need to let your mate know the secret word, use the numbers instead of the letters. You can either make the whole sentence into numbers or just the super-secret words! So, if you wanted to tell her about your 'sleepover' that would be 8, 15, 22, 22, 11, 12, 5, 22, 9.

IT'S PERFECT FOR WHEN YOU'RE TEXTING OR EMAILING AND DON'T WANT ANYONE TO FIND OUT WHAT YOU'RE TALKING ABOUT!

A	26
B	25
C	24
D	23
E	22
F	21
G	20
H	19
I	18
J	17
K	16
L	15
M	14
N	13
O	12
P	11
Q	10
R	9
S	8
T	7
U	6
V	5
W	4
X	3
Y	2
Z	1

It's Elemental

Fire
Aries, Leo and Sagittarius

Personality: You're a bit of a chatterbox and you just have to be in on the latest gossip and giggles. But you're great at keeping secrets too and you often know more than people guess! You love a challenge and you're always on a mission; even tiniest sniff of an adventure is enough to get you going. But watch how you go, cos you can be a teensy bit clumsy!

Friendship rating: You're a generous friend and you're loads of fun to be around.

Most likely to say: 'Follow me, everybody!'

Water
Cancer, Pisces and Scorpio

Personality: You're a sensitive, artistic kind of girl who loves getting creative. You can be a teeny bit messy too so there's bound to be a few splodges of paint on your bedroom carpet. You're a bit of a fashion guru and you've got a real talent for picking out clothes and mixing up your styles. You've got a sweet nature and you love helping people out when you can.

Friendship rating: You're a great listener and a truly loyal mate.

Most likely to say: 'Express yourself!'

What secrets can your star sign element reveal about your personality?

Air

Gemini, Libra and Aquarius

Personality: You're an original thinker and you've got bags of imagination. You're also pretty well balanced and a great judge of character. But you can be a teensy bit emotional! In fact, it's not safe to leave you in front of a nature programme without a family-sized box of tissues. Watching orphaned baby animals is all too much for a sweetie like you!

Friendship rating: Your mates love you because you're so much fun.

Most likely to say: 'I've got an idea!'

Earth

Capricorn, Taurus and Virgo

Personality: You're a down-to-earth girl and you see things very reasonably. That's means that you're great at sorting out problems and getting things done. But you're not all about the practical stuff. You're also totally caring and considerate. In fact, some people secretly think you're a bit of a psychic because you're so thoughtful and sweet.

Friendship rating: You're fab at making your friends feel special.

Most likely to say: 'Are you OK?'

Megastar

Everyone has blushing blunders – here are some from your Megastar Mystery friends!

Rosie

My mum is in a Bananarama tribute band, and if you haven't heard of them, then all I can say is that you're very, very, very lucky. Anyway, last Saturday, Mum wanted to rehearse and she asked me stand in as a backing singer. Seeing as we were in the privacy of our own home, I decided to help her. Wrong decision. Mum secretly videoed me singing and sent it in to Time Lord to prove that I deserved a singing role in the next school play. He showed it to the entire class. I need to leave the country under an assumed identity. Now!

Paige

I was shopping in the mall when this boy came up to me and gave me a kiss on the lips. I freaked out and totally chopped him with a great move from my karate class. It wasn't until he was rolling around at my feet that I realised he was Shelby's boyfriend. He must have got us muddled up. To make things even worse, the paparazzi turned up and started snapping loads of photos and so our blushes ended up in, like, a zillion magazines.

Cringes

Soph

I was trying on a pile of stuff at my fave charity shop when I found this très chic floral dress. I decided to buy it and went up to pay at the counter. Suddenly, an old lady charged out the changing rooms, dressed in nothing but a grey vest and big pants. She started yelling madly that I'd stolen her dress. Somehow, it must've got under the changing room door and ended up in my pile of clothes. I don't know what was worse, being accused of stealing or having the same dress sense as a 75-year-old . . .

Shelby

Last month, Paige and I were flying to Sydney. When we arrived, we went to get our suitcases from the baggage carousel. As the cases came round, I saw that there were clothes all over the place. I was just saying how totally embarrassing it would be for the person whose suitcase had come undone, when I noticed a familiar-looking top. Then I saw my teddy bear, riding on top of somebody's rucksack with a pair of my knickers on his head. Everyone started laughing and I went as red as a stop sign. We had to wait until everybody had gone before I could rescue my stuff.

Soph's Style Tips

Check out these high-fashion tips from stylish Soph!

For a look that's like, totally *Vogue*, team a pair of skinny jeans with a customised T-shirt.

If you're having a bad hair day, don't panic and stress! Just throw on a funky beret and voilà, you are the height of Parisian chic! Très bon!

It's all about the layers this season! Wear one vest top over the top of another and make sure the one underneath shows at the neckline and hem. Très *Vogue*, darlings!

Make sure you invest in a really good pair of shoes. Every fashionista knows that shoes can make or break an outfit.

If you can't afford top designer clothes, be your own designer and get customising!

NOT SO STYLISH
Rosie's Style Tips

Check out these real-fashion style tips from Rosie

For a look that's, like, totally out of Whitney High's student newspaper, team your school skirt with a school regulation blouse.

If you're having a bad hair day, don't panic and stress! Just get over it. There are more important things to worry about – especially if your mum is in a Bananarama tribute band.

It's all about the jeans this season! Wear just one pair at a time and make sure that your pants don't show over the waistband. So *not* très, très *Vogue*, darlings.

Make sure you invest in a really good pair of trainers. Every fashionista knows that trainers are easier to walk in than heels.

If you can't afford top designer clothes, wear jeans!

What's Your

Would you be a show-stopper or a celebrity stropper? Try this quiz to find out!

Q1:
What's more important before a show – learning your lines or getting your hair right?
a. Hair
b. Lines

Q2:
Which of the following do you prefer?
a. Getting loads of attention
b. Being part of a team

Q3:
'I spend ages getting ready for school in the morning.' How true of you is this statement?
a. That's so me!
b. That's so not me!

Q4:
How would your best friend describe you?
a. The life and soul of the party
b. Très helpful and hardworking

Showbiz Style?

Q5:

I think people should . . .
a. Always do what I tell them to do
b. Keep it real

Diva Queen

Lock up your Chihuahuas, Hollywood! Diva queen coming though! Given half the chance, you'd have an entourage big enough to fill a double-decker bus. And why not? It's all about you, right? There's just no point being a star if you don't get star treatment.

Most likely to say: 'It's terribly hot under these studio lights. Could you come over here and fan me? And while you're at it, could you peel me a grape?'

Screen Dream

You'd have to get a good agent because the phone would never stop ringing, girl! Directors would love you because you'd be so easy to work with. And audiences would adore your girl-next-door vibe. You'd be a total Hollywood honey.

Most likely to say: 'Hang on, I just want to go and have a chat with my fans. They've been waiting in the rain for ages.'

Q6:

What would you say if you won an award?
a. 'I couldn't have done it without my friends.'
b. 'I've worked soo hard for this.'

Over-keen

You're a hard-working girl and you take your dreams very seriously. Given half the chance, you'd be learning the lines of your next script before you'd filmed the last scene of your latest movie. If you were famous, you'd spend your entire life trying to be the best in the biz.

Most likely to say: 'If I don't take a break between films, I can be in at least ten movies this year.'

Fact File

NAME: Paige Sweetland

AGE: 16

STAR SIGN: Gemini

HAIR: Dark brown

EYES: Brown

LOVES: Chatting on the phone to her mum

HATES: Matching twin outfits

LAST SEEN: Out shopping for berets with Soph

MOST LIKELY TO SAY: 'Predictions, schmidictions. I'm not sooo into the stars these days.'

WORST CRINGE EVER: Having to re-shoot a TV interview because she had a bogey the size of Hollywood hanging out her nose. Tissue, anyone?

Fact File

NAME: Shelby Sweetland

AGE: 16

STAR SIGN: Gemini

HAIR: Dark brown

EYES: Brown

LOVES: Acting and being an individual

HATES: Dodgy astrologers

LAST SEEN: Hanging out with her mum in a posh London restaurant

MOST LIKELY TO SAY: 'Out with the raisin bagels and in with the bacon sarnies!'

WORST CRINGE EVER: Tripping up on the red carpet, grabbing on to Orlando Bloom in panic and accidentally ripping down his designer trousers. Oops!

Say What?

Check out these top Megastar quotes!

'Sorry! Can't come to watch you practise for the school play, Amanda! Way, way too busy hanging out with the famous Sweetland twins. Byeee!'

Rosie finally gets her own back on annoying Amanda Hawkins.

'I'm getting a very clear vision now. Yes . . . I see . . . a dark room with bars and meals of bread and water. I predict that I will be locked up in prison for a very long time.'

Misty predicts the bloomin' obvious as she's arrested and handcuffed by police.

If you say 'wow' one more time, I'm going to phone up the dictionary people and have it removed from the English language.

Penny finally snaps under the pressure of having Rosie, Abs and Soph to stay.

No, Megan, I don't think that Paige Sweetland wants to play princesses with you.

Poor Abs has yet another intellectual conversation with her five-year-old sister.

'I was totally right! This chambermaid's blouse really does look cool with my jeans! So, the hotel's really gonna miss one little white blouse? Really, Rosie, really?'

How can it be wrong when it looks so right? Sorry Soph, but the blouse is going back!

Rosie's Homework Diary

I actually have to do all of this work by next week; it's sooo not fair!

MONDAY
English: Comprehension thingy

TUESDAY
Maths: Pages 22-26. Five whole pages!
Mr Adams, are you trying to kill us?

WEDNESDAY
Geography: Finish project!!!
What project??? Whoops. Ask Abs.

THURSDAY
None: Yay! →

FRIDAY
History: How the Tudors lived.
What can we learn from an age
when people used to chuck buckets
of wee out of the window instead
of using a toilet like normal people? Discuss.

Abs, Soph –
do you want
to come over tonight
to do some celebrity
sleuthing?

Pam's Problem Page

Never fear, Pam's here to sort you out!

Dear Pam,

Me and my sister are totally obsessed with the stars. What shall we do?

Paige and Shelby

Pam says: Well, dearie, there's nothing wrong with having a hobby. Miss Marple loves her knitting and Jessica Fletcher barely takes a break from her typewriter. Looking up at all the pretty stars is a very nice way to pass the time, except when it's raining. And stars are very useful if you get lost in the woods. I was watching an episode of Miss Marple just the other day and there was a lady who got lost in the woods at night. She found her way out by following the North Star and escaped the mad axeman just in time. So don't you and your sister worry about your little hobby, it may come in useful one day!

Can't wait for the next
book in the series?
Here's a sneak preview of

Angel

Chapter One

Wednesday lunchtimes totally rock.

OK, so I don't usually spend them in the most glamorous location. The third table across from the tray-stack in our grotty school canteen is about as un-glamorous as it gets. But Wednesday is the day my all-time fave celeb gossip mag, *Star Secrets*, comes out each week. Why so marvelloso, I hear you ask?

Top ten cool things about *Star Secrets*:

1. Well, duh – it's full of celeb gossip. I'm not

called Nosy Parker cos I've got a big nose.

2. It's got photos of celebs doing dead ordinary stuff, like emptying the bin in their bunny slippers and no make-up.

3. They have a TV guide that has not been drawn all over in blue biro by my nan, who is obsessed with remembering when her favourite murder-mystery shows are on.

4. The 'Dating or Ditching?' section tells you which stars are going out with each other, so you know which boy-celebs are available and worth fancying.

5. Last week, their astrologer, Destiny Blake, predicted I'd find myself in a sticky situation with a friend. The next day, I sat on a lump of chewing gum on the bus and it went all over the jeans I was wearing, which belonged to Abs. Spooky, eh?

6. They gave the first single by Fusion (lead singer Maff, très gorge singer and co-snogger for my first snog) five stars out of five, which means they have genius taste in music.

7. The fashion pages, titled 'Fashion Passion', are written by it-girl and top style guru, Roma Richie. She's ace. Even Soph agrees.

8. It's about PROPER music – NOT the eighties kind I am forced to listen to at home by Mum.

9. Dreamy boy posters – not only good for delish-ness, but also for covering up the disgusting flowery wallpaper I am not allowed to redecorate in my bedroom.

10. They have interviews with stars full of info on celeb-ness that could be very handy when I am a rich and famous writer.

✳ ✳ ✳

'So, what's new?' said Abs, as I flicked through the glossy pages one particularly gossip-worthy Wednesday lunchtime.

She was sitting opposite me at our usual table, along with my other best mate, Soph, who I knew was itching to get her hands on the mag for the fashion pages.

'Mirage Mullins' new haircut,' I announced. 'Do we like?'

Abs and Soph leaned over to study *Star Secrets'* double-page photo spread of Mirage and her freshly styled choppy bob. Ever since we helped Mirage Mullins out a few months ago, we've sort of felt connected to her, even if she is a mega-successful celeb and we're just three ordinary-ish schoolgirls.

'We like *a lot*,' said Soph. She pulled a strand of her own brown, wavy hair forwards and studied it intently. 'D'you think mine would look good like that?'

'Er, Soph,' said Abs, who was busy investigating the contents of her packed lunch. (Her dad makes these totally random sandwich combos and by the look on Abs's face, today's filling – beetroot, cheese spread and tuna – wasn't going down as an all-time classic.) 'You had to nag your mum for, like, a year before she let you buy hair-straighteners. I don't think she'll be saying yes to blonde highlights and spiky bits any time soon.'

'Hmm,' Soph frowned. She flipped over a few pages of the magazine, still leaning across the table and twirling her hair. 'I do quite fancy a change, though.'

'Look!' I said, suddenly spotting another familiar face as the pages fell open at 'Fashion Passion'. 'It's Angel.'

Soph grabbed the magazine and pulled it across the table to get a better look.

'Model of the moment, Angel, works the red carpet in one of this season's hottest designer trends,' she read aloud from the caption under Angel's photo.

'She looks gorgeous,' said Abs, peering over her shoulder.

'Totally,' I agreed.

'That dress is seriously coolissimo,' breathed Soph.

Angel is a HUGE star. Her real name's Jenny Gabriel and, amazing as it sounds, she was a pupil here at Whitney High until she won a modelling contest last year. Soph is one of her biggest fans.

As she likes to point out whenever anyone mentions Angel (and quite often when they don't), she's proof that fashion dreams really can come true. Angel's younger sister, Francesca, is in Abs's class, so we sometimes get to hear what she's up to. Frankie's almost as gorgeous as Angel herself, but for some très bonkers reason she doesn't fancy a life of glamour, showbiz parties and earning piles of cash for pouting her way down a catwalk. She's planning to be a famous artist instead. I honestly have no idea why anyone would want to spend all day getting paint under their fingernails and then having to cut off their ear or drown half a cow, or any of that weird stuff artists do to get famous. I did quite like the one who didn't make her bed for a whole year and called it art, although there'd be fat chance of getting away with that in *my* house.

'Earth to Rosie. Rosie, this is Earth calling,' I suddenly heard Abs say.

'What?' I said, snapping out of my mini-daydream.

'Duh!' said Soph, pointing down at the mag. It

was now lying open on a page that featured a massivo close-up of Angel's face – the kind of pic that's guaranteed to show up even the tiniest lurking spot and, in my case, that pokey bit of eyebrow that won't lie flat whatever I do to it. 'The new Teen Shimmer colours,' said Soph, still pointing at Angel's face. It was an advert. In one corner of the page, just by Angel's perfectly pointy chin, were the words:

Angel: The Face of Teen Shimmer

Angel wears Emerald City Eye Shine, LushLash Mascara in Chocolate Brown, Cheeky Pink Blush and Pucker Up Glimmer-Gloss, all from the brand new range of Teen Shimmer colours. COMING SOON to a beauty counter near you!

'Just imagine,' said Soph, dreamily, 'being the face of Teen Shimmer. All that free make-up. Every single shade of lippy. Enough nail varnish to paint every one of your fingernails and toenails a different colour . . .'

'Why would you do that?' asked Abs.

'I wouldn't,' said Soph. 'Probably. It's just you'd have enough nail varnish if you wanted to do it.'

'Just think,' I said, 'this time last year, Angel was stuck here, eating lunch in this very canteen, with nothing to look forward to except double science on a Wednesday afternoon. And now look at her.'

'It's like a fairytale,' sighed Soph.

Me and Abs smirked.

'It *is*,' Soph protested. 'She was in this totally cool *Vogue* fashion shoot last month, and she's always doing the big catwalk shows. And we all saw that billboard opposite the bus stop. It was enormous. Her head was about the same size as the bus.'

'A bit like Amanda Hawkins's head, come to think of it,' I said, spotting my least favourite person in the entire world walking across the canteen towards us.

'What's up with you lot?' she snapped, as the three of us collapsed in a fit of giggles.

'Nothing you'd be interested in,' I said.

She threw a haughty glance at the magazine, which was still lying open on the table. 'Jenny Gabriel?' she scoffed. 'You're right – I'm not interested, and I don't know why anyone else is either.'

'Jealous much?' hissed Soph under her breath as Amanda stalked off.

'Course she is,' I said. 'She can't *stand* anyone who gets more attention than her.'

Abs nodded wisely. 'There's your fairytale, Soph,' she said. 'Starring Amanda Hawkins as the wicked witch.'

* * *

By the time I got home that afternoon, I was exhausted. Mum's always moaning about how hard she works at the council offices and OK, she does get home quite a bit later than I do, but at least she doesn't have to sit through French, maths *and* double science on a Wednesday afternoon. Or, for that matter, do homework. Don't teachers realise we have better things to do? Important stuff, like watching *EastEnders* or trying to decide whether Justin Timberlake is cuter than Orlando Bloom. Luckily, just as I was about to start Madame Bertillon's mountain of French homework, Soph's instant-messaging username flashed up on my computer, quickly followed by Abs's, and saved me from death-by-boredom:

FashionPolice: Have you seen latest on the *Star Secrets* website?

CutiePie: Non.

NosyParker: SPILL!

FashionPolice: Très bad. They're saying Angel looks v. thin and is acting weird.

NosyParker: You lie.

FashionPolice: Au contraire, mon doubting frère. Only a rumour, but says she got sent home from a photoshoot last week for acting stroppy.

CutiePie: That so doesn't sound like her.

NosyParker: She was always a real laugh at school.

CutiePie: No way fame would change her that much.

FashionPolice: Or make her lose loads of weight. Stick-thin models are sooo last year.

NosyParker: Has Frankie said anything?

CutiePie: Nope.

FashionPolice: Maybe not true, then.

CutiePie: Rumours suck!

NosyParker: So does French homework.

FashionPolice: Oui, oui, mon amie.

It was pretty weird. I read *Star Secrets* all the time and they're nearly always right, but I totally couldn't imagine Angel throwing a showbiz strop. She was in the year above me, Soph and Abs, but she was always really friendly. We went to Frankie's birthday party one year and Angel was a right laugh. We played loads of really stupid party games, like Sardines and Twister and Murder in the Dark and even though she was older than most people at the party, she joined in with everything and wasn't stuck up at all.

Soph was right, though – it *was* only a rumour. I looked at the stack of French homework sitting on my desk, and tried to put Angel and *Star Secrets* right out of my mind.

As les Français would say, it was très difficile, considering.